ENTER THE QUEEN OF ICE

"Welcome to our little corner of the world," she began, while Hathor stared in awe at her splendid black dress, bejeweled with ice crystals that sparkled and blazed in the torchlight, at her raven hair and luminous black eyes. Regally thin, she was nearly as tall as Hathor, at a third his weight, but a malign strength emanated from her presence, a frosty power that made Hathor shudder involuntarily.

"Are you cold, my warm-blooded one? You better get used to it. Tell us, are there many like you?"

"In some places there are many of my kind," Hathor answered.

"No, no, we mean are there many who are giving up the eating of flesh?"

"No others, that I know of."

"Good. We mean to keep it that way."

Volume Four
HORRIBLE HUMES

Stephen Billias

ACE BOOKS, NEW YORK

This book is an Ace original edition,
and has never been previously published.

RUNESWORD: HORRIBLE HUMES

An Ace Book/published by arrangement with
Bill Fawcett and Associates

PRINTING HISTORY
Ace edition/July 1991

ISBN: 0-441-73697-1

Ace Books are published by The Berkley Publishing Group,
200 Madison Avenue, New York, New York 10016.
The name "Ace" and the "A" logo
are trademarks belonging to Charter Communications, Inc.

PRINTED IN THE UNITED STATES OF AMERICA

10 9 8 7 6 5 4 3 2 1

Dedicated to the memory
of Neal Festinger

CHAPTER
1

A sword. A sword bright and shiny. A sharp, straight sword that sticks and pricks. A hardened, tempered sword, alive and singing, coming at him. And behind it, a hume, a horrible hume, slashing and bashing, thrusting and busting, smashing and attacking.

Hathor clambered awake, chuffing and chumbling, clapperclawing the air in a frenzy with his rough troll's paws. What a terrifying vision had come to him as he slept! Thank the gods it was only a dream, a shade. From the mouth of his cave, dug out of the soft earthen bank, Hathor stared at the River Drasil. Hundreds of years from now this river would silt up and leave him high and dry three miles inland from the sea, in a loamy field of black silty earth, some of the best soil in the realm.

The cave, warm and dank, smelled strongly of Hathor. It stank of Hathor. Hathor did stink, but it was his own good stink, an earthy, fungus-y toadsweat sort of stink, and he didn't mind it, in fact found it comforting.

It's not as bad as before, Hathor thought to himself, when corners of the cave were littered with rotting bones from unmentionable beasts—shoulder of griffon, haunch of hume, disgusting gristly dirt-covered fly-ravaged carcasses—neck of camelopard, *a sweet rare bison roast dripping fat into a hot blaze . . . Ach! No! A plague upon it!*

In his half-waked daze Hathor had momentarily forgotten his vow of vegetarianism. He looked around. The cave was cleared, at least, of bones and hanks of hair and entrails. No longer did Hathor give the "eagle spread" to his adversaries, cutting the lungs from the living victim and spreading his ribs to the sun. No, now he was a peaceful, gentle troll, at least most of the time. But when humes shoved and squeezed him, crammed and jammed him, or if anyone tried to harm his precious charge, the old primitive lust rose up in him like a kettle boiling over, a fearsome frothing frenzy in every direction. Yes, sometimes he slipped, did Hathor.

Ooof! Let others live in the buhrs, behind high dirt ramparts. Hathor preferred his riverside den to the closeness of the walled towns. He preferred the isolation and solitude of subterranean life to the crowds of the streets. And now today, when he had just settled in so comfortably to his buried burrow, and had just shaken off the lingering pains and aches from their last adventure, it was going to start again.

The other three were coming for him today. He would see Bith today. Bith. Whenever Hathor imagined Bith a honey-eyed warmth filled his brain and made his thoughts buzzy and fuzzy like bees in his ears. Good Bith. Sweet Bith. Poor orphaned girl, torn from her palace home. Now everyone she meets is a stranger.

Hathor would watch over her. He had pledged himself to do so, and he did. Indeed, recently there seemed to be times when Bith would have preferred less vigilance from him. But never mind, Hathor decided, as he rummaged and scrummaged through a pile of barely ripe acorns for enough nuts to grind into his morning porridge. "Ach! Life is hard," he grumbled to himself. But outside the bush-shrouded entrance to his damp dark cave, the river flowed on with ceaseless, effortless strength toward the unknown sea. If only Hathor could be more riverlike and less like a clumsy thing with hands of stone. Sometimes Hathor secretly envied the humes, their fair skin and hairless bodies, their hands and feet so delicate even on the ugliest lout among them. But then he would contemplate their other qualities, their greed, rapaciousness, and lust, and he would thank the heavens that he was only an ordinary troll.

And the elf Endril would arrive today, the elf whose name was part of an endless song, of which Hathor had heard only a few short verses, but enough to know that it was magic. For Hathor had a dream, that one day someone, perhaps even Endril, would make a song about him, Hathor, praising his great deeds, hymning his falcon-soaring feats in odes and skalds, immortalizing his name in a hero poem. Someday, when he had deeds enough to sing about.

Cal would be here today too. Young Cal, human Cal. All the things that separated Hathor from the humes were embodied in that impetuous, ardent young man. "Never you mind," Hathor told himself. "There is goodness in Cal, even if at times he goes too far and pushes too hard." Wasn't it he who fought so nobly and killed the demon in the castle in the fight for the sword?

The four of them—Hathor, Bith, Endril, and Cal, each with their own special talents—were a formidable team. But why? What for? Who had chosen them to be false knights, pretenders, serving no king, liegeless, lordless, wandering the barren land at the edge of the Mistwall in search of who-knew-what? The mysterious god Vili, who had appeared to them as a disembodied face in a bucket of water? Was this enough? The hunt for Runesword had nearly cost them all their lives. Then they'd trekked as far as distant Northunderland in search of Skryling's blade Sjonbrand, almost losing both Bith and Endril to the wicked Schlein. Only recently they'd chased all over the Dark Lord's realm after a crystal, on the whim of the sorceress Verna.

And now, some nonsense about a new mission. Just when Hathor had begun to feel at home for the first time in many a long while. Why, to hear the elf tell it, they were all destined for great deeds—perhaps even victory over the mighty encroaching Mistwall itself.

"Fool!" Hathor muttered, referring to himself, not the boastful Endril. Why worry about the murky future when the present was equally foggy? Outside the cave mouth, the morning mist rising off the River Drasil seemed to mock him with its pale echo of the Mistwall. The sun had yet to penetrate the greyness. Hathor couldn't even see across the river to his neighbor Grunold's fields of turnips. Their green, bunchy heads would soon be visible, poking their way out of the silty bottomland across the water and below Hathor's high-riverbank cave.

On sunny mornings the light would stream into the cave mouth, illuminating for a few hours the smoky walls and the piles of rubble, the cobwebs and the chalky dust, the bird droppings and bat droppings that Hathor had become quite used to, but which so distressed rare visitors.

Perhaps I should sweep, Hathor thought to himself, but after a few unenthusiastic efforts he gave up and threw a ragged burlap sack over the worst of the mess.

He gazed hungrily across the River Drasil toward Grunold's turnips, still blanketed in a ghostly pall. Hathor ate turnips raw, munching them with his troll's teeth as if they were apples. Cooking was too much work. And gardening was too much work. Better to forage among the rotting leftovers heaped on Grunold's compost at the raggedy end of the field where the turnip patch ran up against the earthen wall built who-knows-when by who-knows-who to keep the River Drasil in its banks.

But his guests would be here soon, he had no time to ford the river for Grunold's leavings. In fact he had nothing to offer them and could only hope that they had all eaten. Hathor knew that, knowing him as they did, they would understand if he was less than the perfect host. Hathor still had trouble figuring out what he was to eat each day now that he consumed no meat; he was much less ready to prepare victuals for others.

Now, what was that whistling and humming outside his cave mouth? It must be the elf Endril.

"Hallo, there!" Hathor cried out, knowing that the elf would wait outside, peering into the dim interior, rather than crashing in on a troll. One never knows about trolls in their lairs, does one? Hathor followed this prudent practice, even when visiting his own relatives. "Coming! Coming!" Hathor gazed lovingly at the comfortable confines of his cave, then threw on his heavy cloak, crammed his hat on his disheveled hair, and shambled out to meet the first arrival.

Endril was standing on one foot, clapping his diminutive hands to some unheard rhythm, and prancing slowly around and around, his upraised leg kicking in and out.

"What sort of nonsense is this?" Hathor demanded. "You wouldn't be casting spells on my very threshold, would you?"

"Verily, I would," the slim, spritely creature responded. "And you need 'em too."

"What spell is that?" Hathor grumbled, for he distrusted Endril's magic, though it had saved his life more than once.

"The Incantation for Removal of Stink!" the sprite shouted gleefully. "It smells quite shameful right hereabouts."

Just in front of the cave mouth (from which did issue forth the reek of Hathor, there was no denying it) was a small flattened clearing, before the riverbank sloped sharply away to the water. Hathor had dragged two charred logs into the spot for benches, bounding a ring of blackened sooty stones where in the old days Hathor would have roasted meat or dried the skins of his kills. Now the fire pit contained only the husks of a few strange vegetables Hathor had learned to bury in the coals of a fire, then scrape clean of char and devour.

"Charming place you have here," Endril commented wryly as he finally stopped spinning around and placed his other foot back on the ground and faced Hathor directly.

"I like it," Hathor grunted. He was used to the jibes of his companions.

"I see no preparations for leaving. Have you forgotten that today is the day we depart?" Endril wanted to know.

"I have my hat on my head and my cloak on my back. I am ready," Hathor replied gruffly. "What more I need I find as we go." It seemed to Hathor that he could think the human language more clearly than he could speak it. Sometimes when Hathor listened to humans talk, he thought they must be singing to each other, so musical and sweet were the sounds they made. By comparison, the language of trolls was like the grunting of pigs, or like rubbing rough stones together, graceless and hard on the ear. By common consent they spoke the language of men, even when Bith and Cal weren't present. But Hathor always felt tongue-tied in conversation with the glib and jocular Endril.

"And the others? They know to come here?"

"They know."

"You have picked out a path for us to begin the journey?" Endril depended on Hathor as a woodsman and trail guide; Hathor was pleased by the responsibility and prided himself in never getting lost.

"I have. Through the Warding Woods and along the northern edge of Haukslake."

"Good. Then let us sit and wait for the others. Might there be a crust of bread in the larder?" Endril hinted broadly, though he wasn't really hungry, he just wanted to tease Hathor a bit more, and the troll knew it too.

"Bread? I never make bread. Don't know how. There might be a bit of cold acorn porridge left."

"Porridge? I never eat porridge"—the elf wrinkled his dainty nose in disdain—"especially not *cold* porridge."

"I'm sorry," Hathor said, resigned to suffering the jests of his comrade.

"Never you mind," Endril said as he clapped Hathor's broad back with his wee palm, "we're all very proud of you and your new ways. It's not easy for anyone to change for the better. It's much easier to grow worse."

Hathor grunted assent but said nothing.

"Actually, I've a bit of dried fruit here, if you're interested," Endril offered, but Hathor shook his head no. Secretly he was imagining the apple trees on the abandoned farm in the Warding Woods. Once a great landowner's estate, it was now forsaken, the humans long gone, the fields fallen fallow, and the land slowly reverting to forest as it will. The orchard, however, faithfully produced a crop of healthy apples every year, to the delight of the birds and the squirrels and the tiny pronghorn deer and the local elves. The path to Haukslake passed right along the edge of this property, and Hathor hoped for a feast of apples. It was the right time of year, late summer, before the first frost. Hathor was saving his knowledge of the apple orchard as a surprise for his comrades, so he said nothing to Endril, but instead asked about the journey.

"Where are we bound this time, Endril?"

Instead of answering directly, the elf stood up, pulled a handsomely carved flute from the rucksack slung over his shoulder, and trilled a few shrill notes as introduction before singing this song:

"Many kennings know I now, but will make glorious more
To tell the deeds of the mighty troll Hathor,
Whale-hearted, giant slayer, sharp straight axe-thrower,
Foe-felling, enemy-knelling, the noble rescuer."

Endril glanced over to see how Hathor liked his song, which broke the mood of course because Hathor saw at once that the elf was making fun of him. For Endril knew of Hathor's longing for a skald to be sung in his honor in the halls of a great king.

"What is sung in play now may one day come to pass," Endril intoned mock-solemnly, "for verily it is said, 'The fool who persists in his foolishness becomes wise.' "

"Di'ye think me a fool, then, Endril?"

"Aren't we all a little bit so?" the sham philosopher replied. Endril took up his flute and began to play. Hathor noticed it was decorated with two carved snakes entwined between the open holes where Endril placed his fingers to make the different pitches. As Endril played, the snakes seemed to writhe and slither along the length of the slim instrument, but it was only the way Endril swayed and twisted as he blew.

As Endril played, a stamping was heard over the soothing melody of the wind-created music, a tromping and stomping, roughly in beat with the music, as Cal tripped down the footpath from the upper level to Hathor's bankside clearing.

Endril switched to a flute imitation of a horn fanfare, a mocking musical welcome. Cal played the part by taking off his plain round leather squire's hat as if it were a plumed feathered banded royal's headpiece and bowing deeply from the waist.

"Sir Cal at your service, sirs." He was handsome enough to be a knight, except perhaps for the scar above his left eyebrow, but that slash gave him a dashing look, tempered only by the obvious youthfulness of his face, his scraggly beard, and his still bright and eager eyes. He had a look about him that said, "This is me, Cal, this is who I am, and I'm proud of it."

Hathor, more naturally reserved (as a creature who lives in caves and under bridges is wont to be), sometimes found this, and other hume traits, disturbing, but he forced himself to remember that it was merely a different custom, not a matter for hate and loathing. He put out a meaty troll's paw, and did not draw back when Cal clasped him by the wrist.

"Hathor, you old dog, how are you?" Cal shouted in his face and grinned enthusiastically. Hathor bristled because he didn't like the comparison, but he knew Cal meant nothing by it, so he gritted his ugly troll's teeth and grinned back, more like a grimace but the best he could do.

"Hallo, Cal."

Hathor was relieved when Endril ceased his playing to greet the new arrival.

"Cal, laddie, you've grown another inch or two since I saw you last. Perhaps you're even taller than Bith now," Endril teased him, for no one was immune to the elf's sharp tongue.

"If she hasn't shot up another half foot. Isn't that bean-pole ever going to stop growing?" Cal answered heartily, though in her presence he wouldn't have dared talk that way. "What grand and glorious adventure does fate have planned for us this time?" Cal asked Endril, for like Hathor he was respectful of the elf's powers of foresight.

"Keep talking like that and you'll soon be swinging from the Dark Lord's highest gibbet," Endril replied.

The faint scar above Cal's left eyebrow blushed briefly like a crimson caterpillar. "Why?" he wondered, stung by the vehemence of Endril's retort.

"Because we are not adventurers. Our purpose is serious. Our goals are noble, not whimsical. And our desires are not for greater glory for ourselves," and here he gave Hathor a look that made the poor troll feel as if the elf were reading his mind, "but for the improvement of the lot of all beings, and toward the eventual destruction or defeat of the Mistwall that has so intruded into our lands and our lives, choking everything in its poisonous mist."

"Well put, elf." Cal felt sufficiently chided. He jumped up onto the largest rock in the stone fire ring, a four-foot boulder blackened by log ends propped against it. "But if excitement attends our way betides, and fighting and feasting and wooing of maids, we'll not say no, will we?!"

"We'll not, indeed. But it is good to remember that those are the spoils of victory, not victory itself." Endril could not resist getting in the last word. Though tall for an elf, the slender Endril was smaller than Hathor, though none of them would cross him, as they had all witnessed his superbly effortless swordplay.

Hathor had thought that the elf was jesting with his incantation, but suddenly a sweeter fragrance wafted through the clearing. Or was it just his imagination that the sun pierced the ashen mist and the air became perfumed just as Bith clambered down the path from the upper bank.

The three of them rose to welcome their princess. "Bith! Bith!" Hathor cried out, but then he didn't know what else to say and fell silent. Cal doffed his cap again, this time in humility. Endril paid her the honor of not immediately insulting her.

"Greetings, all. I've important news. There's a rift in the Mistwall!"

"At Dripping Hall in the country of the Wind-Websters." Endril revealed his foreknowledge of the event. Hathor too knew that the north country was their destination, by the route Endril had asked him to plan, and other signs he did not mention yet. Cal pretended he knew too, though he hadn't. Bith was disappointed.

"Who told you?" she asked petulantly.

"The Wind. Who told you?"

"A traveler at the Stag's Leap Inn."

"A traveler, eh? That's bad. That means word is getting out. This could be a disaster. We should leave at once." Endril spoke rapidly and without emotion, but the group sensed his urgency. Each attended to their preparations, and within a few minutes they assembled again by the fire ring. Each of them carried a weapon and each wore a rucksack or shoulder-slung bag with a few supplies and possessions. As if by unspoken agreement each stood at one of the cardinal directions, Bith to the north, Hathor to the east, Cal to the west, and Endril to the south. Facing each other across the pit, each raised their weapon—Bith her decorated knife, Cal his plain sword, Hathor his axe, and Endril his delicate deadly slim sword.

"Let us take an oath, then," Endril suggested, and as he spoke fire sprang up in the pit of its own accord, but it was a cold, cold fire.

"We took a pledge when we first met," Cal reminded the grim-faced elf.

"Then let us renew our vows, for steadfast constancy like life itself must needs have nourishment and affirmation to grow and prosper." Following Endril's lead the other three stretched out their free hands and clasped them over the glowing coals and bathed in the bluish flame.

"By our will and the gods' graces may we succeed in our task—" Endril began solemnly, but Cal broke in rudely:

"What is our task? Nobody has said yet."

"All in good time, my brash young friend. To have true faith, to swear an oath, you need not know why you swear or to what you pledge yourself. That is the measure of commitment. You swear to do bidding against unknown dangers. You place at risk your honor, that invisible shield that separates you from all those to whom such ideas have no meaning. Are you willing to do so?"

"I am," Cal said, "but—"

"No buts—your vow entire or none at all."

"You have it." Cal was stunned by the elf's sudden, almost ferocious seriousness. Endril had accomplished his purpose; he had made them all instantly aware of the grave and high nature of their imminent journey.

That settled, Endril continued the oath: "By mighty Othin, and beautiful Freya, and even Vili, who comes and goes, we four do devote ourselves to this our sacred trust, this journey, this calling, this endeavor."

The flames leapt up but did not sear them, then subsided with an audible whisper, as if an unseen presence sighed.

"Now," Cal demanded, "what is our mission that I have blindly agreed to?"

"I have no idea," said Endril.

"What?"

"None at all. Not a thimbleful."

"No visions? No revelations? Nothing?"

"I really haven't the foggiest."

"I do," Hathor grunted.

"You?" Cal scoffed. "Hathor, not to be rude, old guy, but your powers of vision are suspect."

"Wasn't it I who knew there were wormholes in the castle mountain at Cairngorm?" Hathor defended himself, for sometimes he truly did know things, though he knew not how he knew.

"Exactly!" Cal rejoined. "And didn't those wormholes almost get us killed? They did."

"What is it that you think you have divined," Endril asked Hathor softly, as Cal's ribbing had vexed the ornery troll.

"It has something to do with the tear in the Wall, of which I knew before Bith announced it."

"How can we be sure of that?" Cal demanded to know.

"Because I told you so," Hathor answered indignantly. One did not doubt the integrity of a troll. A troll might be a hume-eater, a devourer of raw flesh, even a cannibal, but his word was good. And he was their boon companion, a good troll with eccentric vegetarian tastes. His word was not to be questioned.

"We all know that now, Cal," Endril intruded on the argument, which threatened to turn ugly. "The question is, what does it all mean? Is the tear to let something in or let something out? What is our role in the unfolding drama? Why has each of us, except, it seems, Cal," Endril said pointedly, putting the overeager young man in his place for Hathor's benefit, "discovered the news separately, by whatever means?"

"We must go there to find out," Cal suggested.

"*Ipso facto, quid pro quo*, and *pro nobis bonum*, young comrade. You've hit the nail on the head."

"Let's go then!" Cal shouted, and with that he hoisted his pack on his shoulder. And so, early on a peaceful summer's morn, the four, bonded by a sacred oath and sworn to each other's fealty, forded the misty River Drasil and began the long walk to Dripping Hall in the north country, the land of the Wind-Websters and the rumored rent in the once-invulnerable Mistwall.

CHAPTER
2

So off they went, the four of them sloshing through the pebbly rapids of the River Drasil, up the far bank, past Grunold's fields, and on into the first scrubby outlying trees of the Warding Woods. The forest was so huge that towns on one side did not even trade with towns on the other—the journey was considered too risky for commerce. No road through the woods ever remained open, though several had been built, all along the same corridor, following a streambed through the center of the woods. It was along this latest abandoned thoroughfare, already nearly obliterated by new growth, that the four struggled as they entered the thicker portion of the forest. It was known to be at least seven days' walk to the north end of the woods from the south end where they had entered. Deep in the woods now, the four were used to the silence and the rhythmic sounds of each other's footsteps. They knew the forest, each of them, though none as deeply as Hathor, for this was his territory, his land for roaming in the gloaming. It was he who showed them the way, sometimes leaving the stream to climb a small knob and scout ahead, sometimes leading them across the flow, sometimes above it, and sometimes wading through it waist deep between steep walls, and riding the rapids on their backsides down rocks worn smooth by centuries of water ceaselessly scouring them.

The first night they camped under the stars. Hathor would have preferred the damp overhang beneath the streambed, but he acquiesced to a patch of ground above the creek. Bith complained of sore feet. Cal sharpened his sword. Endril played his pipes, and each of them fell asleep dreaming of the days to come and the unknown adventures that awaited them.

They reached the abandoned estate late in the afternoon of the second day. The castle itself was long since ransacked, burned to the foundation, and forsaken. The break in the canopy of leaves afforded by the ruins was welcomed by all four of the weary travelers. "Slogging through that streambed is hard work," Cal griped.

"That's nothing to what we have ahead. A day farther the streambed gives out and we must climb the ridge, past the height where the trees cease to grow and each step is a considered risk," Endril commented wryly, before Hathor had a chance to open his mouth. "Let's gather up some firewood. We can rest here for the night and tackle the ridge crest in the morning." As usual, the elf made the decisions for the group, for he was the true leader, even if Bith thought she was because she was a princess and Hathor thought he was because he was the strongest and knew the woods the best and Cal thought he was because he was the bravest and the boldest.

Hathor left the group in the clearing. He poked around a bit as if he too were gathering wood, then set off down a faintly marked path off the main trail toward what he hoped was the forgotten baronial orchards.

Secretly he was discouraged that his leadership was obviously not as valuable as he had thought to the prescient elf. *At least I can bring them something to eat this time*, he thought as he ambled down the concealed brush-covered path toward the orchards.

The rippling outline of a shadow across the clearing was the first warning the others had. Almost before Bith could shout aloud, the immense form of a dragon loomed over them, claws outstretched, nostrils flaming, scaly tail swinging left and right behind its mighty wings. Instead of assailing them, however, the dragon held back, as if trying to identify its prey more clearly before the kill, so as not to eat anything distasteful, perhaps.

"Why doesn't it attack?" Cal shouted to Endril, who was caught without his bag of tricks and momentarily was thinking only of how to save his own elfskin. The dragon spiraled above them, occasionally venting its apparent anger with steaming puffs of smoke, but no fire.

"I feel like the mouse that a cat toys with," Endril admitted. Although he had crawled closer to his bag, he dared not cross the final few steps to retrieve it.

"Look, it's trying to tell us something." Bith, with her intuitive powers, recognized the animal's attempt to communicate. The three heroes gave off scrambling for their weapons and watched in awe as the dragon put on an aerial display the like of which they had never seen.

The dragon dipped and swerved, puffing and belching as he flew, until the name HATHOR was clearly spelled out in plumes of smoke that hardly drifted in the still air, and hung as an ominous cloud over their heads. The dragon hovered beneath his handiwork as if waiting for an answer.

"What do you suppose it means?" Bith wondered.

"And where is that bedeviled troll, anyway?" Cal demanded, as for the first time they noticed his absence.

Did the dragon have him? Was that the meaning of the message? Or, worse, was the dragon looking for him? Endril decided to find out which was which.

"I am Hathor," he said simply. In response, a straight focused flame shot from the mouth of the dragon and exploded where Endril had been standing until an instant ago when he jumped sideways with all the fleetfootedness he could muster.

Before a second bolt could issue from the dragon's mouth he shouted: "No, No! I am not Hathor!" and the perplexed beast hesitated an instant, which was long enough for Endril to have lined up a shot at the stationary dragon. The arrow caught the animal in its reptilian jaws and pierced its small brain, killing it instantly. It fell from the sky like a stone and crumpled in a heap near the pile of wood they had gathered.

"That takes care of *that*," Cal said smugly.

"Not quite," said Endril, and he pointed wordlessly in the direction the dragon had arrived from.

Behind the dragon came a flight of the feared foedingbats, terrifying flying rodents with teeth like saber-toothed tigers', red gleaming eyes, and flat snouts like boars. Hundreds of them darkened the sky, their wings spread to a yard and more, blotting out the dragon's sky-scratching smoke with their flapping leathery appendages.

"Watch out!" Cal cried, but it was too late, a jaws-open foedingbat came screaming at Bith from behind, intent on her fair neck. She ducked at the last minute and the bat's claws caught in her hair, the nightmare of every country girl. She screamed and waved her dagger wildly, nearly stabbing herself in an ear in her panic. Cal leapt from the stone wall a good twenty feet to Bith's side, swinging his blade as he jumped, slicing off the foedingbat's head and a length of streaming red hair, just as the foedingbat's gaping jaws searched hungrily through Bith's tangled hair for her pale nape. As he freed her from this fright, Cal was struck full square in the back by an attacking bat, knocking him facefirst into the ground.

"I think I've broken my nose!" he shouted, but no one was listening, as each of them was busy fending off three or four or a dozen diving, swooping creatures. The sight of blood streaming from Cal's nostrils further whipped up the feeding lust of the already delirious foedingbats. Forty of them rushed at Cal's face at once, and only their ineptness, greedily crashing into each other in their efforts to be the first to rip at his bleeding face, saved him from being slashed up by their vicious fangs. He backed up against a wall and urged his comrades to do the same, as the bats then had to swoop to avoid the wall and couldn't attain full speed in their charges.

Bith tried a "FREEZE" on them but the enraged bats came on, becoming perhaps even more frenzied as they felt the invisible waves of magic striking them harmlessly.

Only when Hathor arrived, swinging a pitchpot of smoking black cedar drip, did the fury of the bats abate. He assaulted them recklessly, as if to make up for his absence at the beginning of the attack. Using the pitchpot as a whirling ball and chain he lashed into the air, smashing the disoriented bats out of the sky as they flew. Bith, Cal, and Endril had to duck for cover as fiery pitch flew in all directions out from where Hathor stood, flailing away at the circling foedingbats. Here and there small fires sprang up as the pitch struck ground kindling, and soon the battle area lay in a pall of smoke and the bats, though they flew without using their eyes, were nonetheless stunned by inhaling the thick smoke, became dizzy, and finally flew off in frustrated and much-depleted disorder.

"Sorry to have deserted you," Hathor said sheepishly as he stood in the midst of the smoking ruins of the ruins. "If I'd have been here at the first—"

"If you'd have been here at the first we'd all be dead now, for the dragon would not have hesitated—it was after you, you know."

"Dragon?! Me?!" Hathor protested. "There are no dragons in Warding Woods, or this whole part of the country, nor have been, for many years now."

"Tell that to the rib roast over there," Cal sniffed. A splash of pitch had ignited the loose-lying gathered logs near the fallen reptile, and its left side was now basting nicely against the flames.

"We'll feast tonight, won't we, eh? They say the flesh of a dragon makes women more beautiful and men more virile," Cal boasted, forgetting that Hathor would not be partaking.

"I—I've brought you some apples," Hathor said feebly. His special treat now seemed insignificant in comparison to the undeniably tantalizing aroma of dragon meat.

"Wonderful!" said Endril. "These will keep much better on the road than meat, which goes green in a few days."

"Unless you salt it up and dry it 'til it's practically leather," Cal added, and he wandered over to the fire to see if he could make the dragon cook more evenly.

"So what did the dragon want with you?" Endril asked Hathor.

"There are no dragons—" Hathor began again, but it was useless, the evidence lay smoking and broiling just a few feet away from him. "I don't know," was all he could reply.

"This journey begins inauspiciously. I fear that if we had left a day later, our attackers would have caught us in the open, or, worse yet, at our very starting point. I ask each of you again—you told no one of our departure?"

"None—except that stranger at the inn," Bith admitted.

"The stranger again." Endril made a face. "Well, what do you think, Hathor, should we stay here the night or push on, now that we know we are pursued, though we know not why?"

"We can't leave now," Cal protested. "This dragon's still half raw."

"I'd rather have a wall at my back tonight, and a bright blaze for company, than dark woods," Hathor said firmly.

"We're all agreed," Endril rejoined.

"No!" said Bith, who was the last to emerge from her hiding place after Hathor's rescue. "Suppose the bats come back again? I—I'm frightened!" she admitted, and her pale face shone even paler, like the moon in a noon sky.

"As long as the fire burns they'll keep their distance," Endril assured her. "Come then, I'll wash and cut your hair so as to even things out. Your previous barber left something to be desired."

Bith's hair was indeed chopped raggedly where Cal had slashed at the foedingbat, and stained with the creature's thick blood. She was a sight. Endril knew that some cleaning up would do much toward restoring the girl's shattered spirits.

"Alright," Bith said dully, and Endril guided her off. It was shocking to see the usually imperious and demanding erstwhile princess being led docilely away.

Hathor had wandered away to the smoldering dragon's form. He stood silently over it, rocking back and forth as if to some unheard music. Cal approached him with a playful greeting.

"I think I like her better that way, what do you think, old fellow?"

"Go away." Something in Hathor's voice made Cal take a step back. He had spoken in troll instead of hume, but Cal knew a word or two of it, and in any case Hathor's tone of voice carried sufficient warning.

"I claim this as my kill," Cal protested, but from the glaze in Hathor's eyes Cal could see that the blood gorge had risen in him, that apples were not going to satisfy him tonight. "But never mind about that—surely you'll share some with your comrades?" Cal asked.

"Eat apples, or bats," Hathor answered. "This"—he gestured heavily toward the roasting dragon carcass—"is mine."

"Will you eat the whole beast then, you trollish glutton, or is it gluttonish troll, I don't know," Cal spoke nervously, still hoping to prevent what he knew was about to take place. It was useless. Hathor dragged the half-raw, half-burnt carcass away from the flames and into the bushes.

"Well, I suppose broiled bat wouldn't be half-bad at that," Cal decided, talking to himself in the empty clearing, and he set about skinning one of the horrid-looking creatures. From the nearby thicket came the unmistakable crunching and gnawing of bones. Poor Hathor had sunk into carnivorism again.

CHAPTER
3

The next morning Hathor was execrably miserable. He was ashamed to show his face and had to be called out of the underbrush by Endril when it was time to leave. Cal still hoped there might be something left of the dragon to take with them, but Hathor soon made it clear that there was not a scale, not a claw, not a dragon's knuckle to be had. He had eaten it all.

Bith too was a little bit abashed. Cal complimented her on her new look, but she was unused to the lighter head that her shorter hair gave her. It made her almost dizzy, and she felt weak, though that was understandable as they had been through quite a fight the day before. The ground was still littered with dead bats. All of the travelers wished to put the horror of the previous day behind them, so it was early that morning when Endril coaxed Hathor from his hiding place. The wretched troll was hopelessly disconsolate. He had deprived his fellows of food and also broken a vow he had made to himself. For the next week, he would eat nothing but bark torn from tree trunks, as tough as—well—as tough as tree bark.

The creek they had followed for two days gave out in a tangle of thorny woldrose and nettles. Though they probed left and right, the travelers could not find a break in this patch of thorn bushes. In order to move forward they had to hack away at the thickly overgrown woods, not at all like the high-canopied pine stand of soft and clear forest floor that Hathor remembered as being here at the end of the creekbed. Was he lost, on top of his other misfortunes?

"Listen!" Endril entreated them, and all stopped their laborious flailing at the dense vegetation.

"What is that sound?" Cal asked for he heard it too, a thudding, then a crackling, repeated, a thud and then a crackle, growing and joining the previous crackles in a chorus. Now they all heard it, all around them, and moving ever closer to them.

"The forest—it's growing in on us," Bith whispered, yet she was strangely calm, considering her fright of the day before. When Endril made a hushed remark to that effect, she said simply, "This is magic I understand."

Cal, when he realized what the sound was, redoubled his efforts to chop his way through the maze of thorns, but now as soon as he severed a limb a new bush would break from the woodland soil with a thud and begin to grow at an astonishing rate. Hathor too swung his axe but to little effect. Who knew how far in all directions this wicked barrier had sprung up? Surely Bith was right, this was magic. But did she have the magic to counter it?

The thorn bushes began to grow so fast and so nearby they were soon pressing in on the four, who anon had their backs to each other and were all slicing away at the infiltrating barbs and stickers of the thorns. The horrendous crackling sounded like a fire, but it was the new branches of the invading wood popping out of their new-formed trunks. Endril was so busy hopping from one foot to the other as he swung his rapier, he barely had time to shout from the side of his mouth to Bith: "Do something!" before a new-grown pricker sprouted almost into his short wispy beard.

Bith clutched the purple stone dangling from the leather thong around her neck. Summoning her strength, she disappeared inside herself to reach the place where, in her childhood, magic had been entrusted—great magic, greater than she knew or remembered, except in times like these. With her eyes closed and the vines and thorny spines threatening to strangle or mangle her, she uttered one word: "FREE!"

At once the thorny jungle parted and the four of them ran through the sudden gap into a pleasant glade of pine and cedar. When they looked back in amazement, the thorns were receding like a wave into nothingness. Soon they could see nothing but friendly forest all around them. They were where they were supposed to be. The murderous thicket where they had been just before no longer existed—it had been an illusion, placed there by an unknown foe. Someone or something knew they were coming and did not want them to reach their destination, that much was clear.

This attack was indiscriminate. The next one was not. It came on the fourth day as they crested a small swale in the center of the pine forest known as Knudson's Knoll, which offered a vantage point from its east side all the way to the Sea of Storms, whose coastline they would follow north. Although it would take them another three days to walk the intervening miles, somehow it was reassuring to be able to see their immediate aim, the distant shore of the sea, not actually visible but marked by the dense natural fog that clung to its edge.

" 'Tis a beautiful morn," said Endril as they all stood facing east on an outcropping of tumbly boulders near the low hill's summit. He thought of playing a daybreak tune to the sun, which was just then shedding the shroud of the coastal fog and rising free into the blue.

"Yes," said Cal, "look at that flock of birds catching the morning updrafts. Wish I could soar like that."

"What kind of birds are those?" Bith asked, still wary of flying creatures after her encounter with the foedingbats. "I don't recognize them."

Hathor strained his eyes to see their teeming flight, though it was easier now as the mass of winged things was making straight for their position at the top of the mound.

"Those aren't birds, they're slizards," Hathor shouted, naming the feared omnivorous reptilian creatures that flew, swam, and crawled in swarms. "Down everybody!"

Bith screamed and huddled hugging herself under the nearest boulder while Hathor, Cal, and Endril prepared to fight, but the slizards ignored the other two and charged Hathor, screeching his name between their rows of tiny sharp teeth as they came. The first assault missed him by inches as he crouched between two rocks. Like the foedingbats, the slizards came in too fast and too close together, cutting down on their effectiveness. Unlike the bats, the slizards were also effective on the ground. A dozen of them fluttered down and landed below the summit, scurrying over the rocky terrain into an immediate fighting posture, their neck hoods swelling and changing colors and their tails swishing nervously behind them.

A leader came forward while the slizards in front preened and postured and the ones in the air circled nastily above the beleaguered band of four.

"Give us Hathor and the rest of you do not die in our jaws or on our claws," he proclaimed.

"What quarrel have you with a peaceful troll?" Hathor asked peevishly. In spite of the danger he seemed to enjoy being the center of attention. "I did not slay your cousin the dragon, I only ate him."

"We care nothing for the dragon. Our master bids us kill you. We obey."

"Who is your master, then?" Hathor asked, but in response the slizard flicked out his long tongue in disdain.

"Enough. What say you, troll? Do you spare your comrades' lives and come to us, or must we fell you all?"

"Damn Knudson and his knoll and all who fall here! You must try!" Cal shouted bravely, and Hathor's gratitude shone in his open face. From her hiding place Bith hissed at Endril, who also stood nearby, challenging the slizard horde.

"Tune them a lullaby, Endril," Bith ordered, and luckily Endril knew what she meant. In an instant he took his flute out of his bag and began piping an eerie melody, swaying as he played. The slizards immediately began to undulate in rhythm to the sinuous notes, and they involuntarily drew closer to the sound. They lost their fearsome aspect—their tongues lolled out of their jaws and their eyes, already sleepy-looking with their hooded sheaths, grew even more drowsed. In a moment they were sleepwalking.

"Wonderful," Cal whispered, none too loudly for fear of waking them. "We could slaughter them all."

"Better to flee now and leave them behind," Endril said curtly, for it offended his sense of fair play to think of taking advantage even of slimy creatures like the slizards.

"How did you know, Bith?" Endril asked, but the high-strung princess demurred to answer. It was enough that she had remembered the trancing effect wind music would have on the slizards.

"Three creatures of the north, the dragon, the foedingbats, and the slizards, all far out of their element, all determined to stop us, or at least Hathor, from reaching that for-lorn region. Why? Hathor, do you have some secret quest that we should know of that may be subtly influencing our fate?"

Endril posed this question to Hathor after they had tiptoed between the subdued slizards and left Knudson's Knoll far behind, plunging back down the hill and into the protective covering of the forest. Once they had put some distance between themselves and the Knoll, Endril had suggested a rest, and queried Hathor, not privately but in the presence of the other two, who also reclined exhausted against near-by trees.

"I ask this question openly, because it affects us all. These creatures definitely had you in mind, and not for the exchanging of pleasantries, apparently. Now, is there anything you want to tell us?"

"I have no secrets," the honest troll replied. "I only wish to know—why I still crave flesh, hume flesh—I am shamed to say this before the two humes among us—why is the flesh of humes so sweet—how I can keep from falling into that horrible habit again—that's all—but what could that have to do with the Mistwall or anything else?" Hathor cried out in anguish, these few troubled phrases the longest speech he had ever made.

"Alright, old friend, alright, calm yourself. We all understand how hard it is for you—still, there can be no doubt of the connection, can there?"

"None." Bith spoke up with firmness. "There is something I didn't tell you. When the slizards were falling asleep, I saw their collective dream. A dragon, huger by far than the one Cal slew, stood guardian of the castle lair of some evil lord, whose face I could not see. It is to this unseen lord of death that all the creatures of the Underworld who have been assailing us owe allegiance."

"Are you sure?" Endril questioned her closely, for the fate of their whole venture might turn on what memories Bith could dredge from her mental contact with the slizards. "Where was this castle? Was it in the north country? We must know!"

"I cannot say. Only, the wind, the wind was flowing in colored streamers—"

"That's it! The country of the Wind-Websters, don't you know? Have you never seen their sky creations?" Endril exulted. Now he was sure he was on the right trail, though the signs had pointed the way right along. Better to be sure than hopeful. "Oh, you will, you will! It's glorious!" And the elf hopped up and down in his excitement.

"I still don't see what all this has to do with me," Hathor groaned.

"Neither do I, old friend, but no matter. We go north. Or rather, to be precise, we continue east until we reach the coast, then north," the meticulous elf corrected himself.

"If these attacks are going to continue, perhaps I should travel alone," Hathor said somberly, for he little wanted to leave his fellows, but desired even less to cause harm to come to them. But none would hear of it, and if anything they wasted useless moments over the next few miles, each one insisting that Hathor walk with *them* for a stretch.

Bith was slowly regaining her princesslike command of herself. Having been the rescuer in the last two episodes with the strangling trees and the slizards, she felt it incumbent upon herself to imagine once again that she was a great magician and that Endril was merely her assistant, when in fact he could spell her under the table, so to speak.

"Come, Endril, let's play at the runes, what do you say?" she challenged him as they walked beneath the sandy pines, the cool sea breeze fluttering in their faces as they neared the shore.

"I never play at magic," Endril answered, which was an innocent falsehood, because in fact the elves are notorious tricksters and pranksters and are always at each other with mischief, but he was trying to set a good example for the talented young girl and did not want her to pick up any bad habits. "You must treat your gift with respect. Otherwise, when the time comes to use it for real, you may not have sufficient bearing to utilize it."

" 'Bearing'! What a funny word. What have bears to do with it?"

"You know what I meant. And besides, as we go into the north country, bears may have a lot to do with it."

"Better a bear than a bat!" Bith replied, still trying to tease Endril into the rune-game, a kind of supernatural poetry competition where the most magical phrase wins.

"Better a bat than an ocecat!" Endril joined the game, because he couldn't resist, and they shot spell-names at each other rapidly like word-warriors.

"Better a rat than a whim and a wending—"

"Better a patch on cloth that needs mending—"

"Furious tigers—"

"Symmetrical spiders—"

"Timorous toads—"

"Vanishing roads—"

"Freya's apron—"

"Vili's vapors—"

To Hathor's crude troll ears the next few words were silver-tongued gibberish, and Cal wasn't paying attention, but if one listened closely one would have heard the two of them chanting in the tongue of the Otherworld, a dialect in which consonants and vowels are never used in the same word, so each utterance is either silvery smooth or choppy, creating a singsong effect that is perfect for the magic it expresses. At the last Endril was victorious with his never-ending supply of mystic verse, of which his name was only the tiniest fragment of a fragment. Bith relented, pouting that she had lost the game she suggested playing, and went off to sulk over her petty defeat. Endril laughed, for it was good training for the girl and in the midst of the competition he had caught a glimpse of the greatness that awaited her in magical maturity. To let her win now would give her a false sense of her progress. Better to let her struggle now, the more surely to vanquish later.

Hathor found himself walking with Cal. It wasn't that he disliked the hume's company—the young man just made him uncomfortable, that was all. Or was it the other way around? Did he worry that now he made Cal uneasy, with his open talk of his problem.

Almost as if Cal were reading Hathor's thoughts, he laughed at the troll: "Why the long face, Hathor? Am I too skinny to make a good meal of?"

"Don't joke," Hathor warned, for he was not in the mood for it. Subsisting on tree bark has a way of souring one's whole outlook on life.

"Fine day, a walk through the forest, the sea and adventure ahead—"

"We're not going to sea again?"

"Probably not. But you never know. Perhaps it would be faster by boat up the coast."

"They don't call it the Sea of Storms for nothing," Hathor grumbled. "I've heard tell of storms where ships were blown a hundred miles inland."

"The remains of one were found on that hill back there," Endril interjected as he caught up to the two of them. "Knudson was a seafaring king from a land even farther to the north of where we go, in that frigid nameless country across the Sea of Storms. He came on a raiding party to pillage the shoreline, but when the storm was through with him, he and his longboat and all his men were aground halfway up that slope, so he settled in right there. Knudson's Knoll."

Hathor liked damp, dark places, not totally wet places. Though he lived near a river, he didn't live *in* the river, nor did he wish to risk his life on the Sea of Storms in a puny rickety concoction of wooden planks caulked together and steered by a stick. That vast expanse of water frightened him. It was too powerful, too unpredictable, too open and limitless, and too much unlike a cozy cave. But if the rest of them insisted, he supposed he would go. He'd caused enough trouble already on this trip.

"Don't brood, Hathor. Tell us your thoughts. Your eyebrows hang as heavy as late-summer thunderclouds," Cal chided and pried, but Hathor remained silent. Then as they walked along Endril cleared his throat and quietly began to tell a story to the young squire and the troll, but Bith caught up so she could listen too, because when an elf spins a story there's usually a weave and a warp and a wisdom way to it.

"Once there was a king of the land where Knudson came from, a land that has known many kings, many races, many invasions, and many sackings and burnings as well. The people there lived in a nearly constant state of war, of preparing for war, or of mopping up the bloody aftermath of war. Consequently, they were a harsh, proud, strong, brutal tribe, these ancestors of Knudson, for we are talking about a time long ago, even before the invasion that brought Knut Knudson to our land—"

"What was their name?" Cal broke in, which you are never supposed to do when an elf is skalding, but instead of insulting Cal, Endril patiently explained that the tribe had no name. It must be a very important story, the three listeners realized, for Endril to suffer an interruption so tolerantly.

"These people existed before the naming of things, when there were only runers and rymers to preserve knowledge from one generation to the next. Singers of songs like myself, indeed, this tale is in my endless song somewhere, but I can't just pull it out for you, so I must paraphrase from memory."

The weary travelers had reached the foot of the coastal hills, where the immense forest finally gave way to scrubby windswept gorse, heather, and occasional patches of wildflowers. As one they sat down on a fallen log at the edge of the forest to hear out Endril and rest before the last ascent to the sea cliff.

"Not only did they not have names for things, they had no names for themselves or each other. They communicated in signs and gestures. When they wanted something, they pointed or just took. What then, you might ask, did the runers rune or the rymers rhyme? Nothing. They were dumb shows! But this did not mean the people did not have voices. Oh, they did, they made the most horrible screams and shrieks and grunts, but none of it had meaning, until one of their gods, a long since forgotten deity whose name does not even exist in our legends, took pity on them and sent a messenger to them with the power of speech in a box.

"This messenger, however, was a prankster named Keymon who had his own ideas about how the people of the north should learn. Instead of showing them the box, he hid it under his vestments and pretended that the words that emanated therefrom were coming from him. Well, as you can imagine, they made this Keymon their first and foremost object of worship, and venerated him most lavishly with food, ale, and other delights. Thus Keymon was not at all anxious to reveal that the power of speech was supposed to be a gift to them. He taught the people the rudiments of language, but withheld from them its more wonderful powers. They knew only the words that enabled them to serve him. He had enslaved them with ignorance.

"Things went on this way for many years, until the unknown god decided to pay a visit to the ancestors of Knudson, to see how they were faring with their newfound tongue. Naturally, when Keymon heard that his master was coming, he panicked. In his rush to avoid detection and punishment, Keymon called all the people together and threw the box among them, then fled. But because they were not taught correctly, each one heard the box just a little differently, and though they all learned how to speak, none could understand the other, and they wandered off, each thinking they had received a wonderful gift but none able to share it with the other. Unable to communicate, they dispersed and formed new tribes, each of which spoke only the way the first of them had heard the speech box. And that is why the tongues of the world today, though related, are all different, and people have so much trouble understanding each other, even when they think they speak the same language."

"Wonderful!" Bith cried, for she more than the others understood the special magic behind that particular story, for she knew that with words you could create light, and effect change—without them there is only darkness and stagnation.

"But what happened to Keymon?" Hathor wanted to know.

"The god caught up to him, of course, and he was given a fitting punishment. He lost his own ability to speak. Everything he uttered came out as a howl or a screech. Imagine how maddening this must have been, for one who was used to conversing freely. Keymon was so ashamed he fled to a strange forest far to the south, and lives there today still, it is said, with a whole tribe of descendants who likewise only shriek and yowl."

"A handsome story," Cal commented, "but what does it have to do with our venture?"

"Ah!" Endril replied, but whether that was a meaningful answer Cal could not be sure, and the mischievous elf would not say.

CHAPTER
4

Far to the north, there was a dragon sentry, and there was a castle, a castle of ice and stone, on a patch of mountainous craggy rock so desolate no one would storm it. If they did, and if they somehow managed to overcome the ferocities of the northern dragon who was not a fire-breather but an icy tempest-tosser, they would find nothing of value for their efforts. The castle was a cave; not a burrow like Hathor's but a magnificent palace, not under the ground but inside the mountain, with gigantic needles of ice as pillars and splendid carved boulders as seats and one enormous rock in particular as a throne in the center of the vast, empty, gleaming chamber, where voices echoed into infinity down unending passageways leading off the central vestibule.

On this chair of power reposed the Queen of Ice who had launched so much trouble toward the four travelers in such a short time. Who was she? What strange fate linked this faraway magician of the ice lands to them? She sat with her back to the dim opening from whence flew her malign flocks. Those were the raiders who had attacked Hathor and his friends, and who kept the few local inhabitants of the region in perpetual fear, always glancing skyward as they tended their meager crops or fished or hunted, always fearing they were about to become prey themselves.

Her face was not visible, but even from the back one could see the cruelty residing in those sharp shoulders, that stiff, proud neck, the pointed ears, and the black-draped royal robes worn so regally, so haughtily. No, one didn't need to see this personage's face to know that evil would show there, in those unseen malevolent eyes.

Nameless and faceless, at the moment she was also enraged, furious that her first assaults had failed. Her nemesis was still approaching, still unaware of the wrath he was bringing upon himself. That troll must die. If all flesh-eating creatures turned to peaceful vegetarian ways, the Queen of Ice would be ruined, her dominion shattered, her gory rule ended. Silent, cold, brooding, the Queen of Ice schemed and darkly dreamed her next vengeful act.

CHAPTER
5

On the seventh day of the journey they reached the Sea of Storms, after an arduous descent of the rock cliff face to the narrow shore. From there the coastline stretched almost unbroken for hundreds of miles to the north, and a good fifty miles to the point at Alemeph. Only an occasional skerry sticking out of the water at low tide, its reeflike rugged bunch of sea rock topped with dead-man's arms of seaweed waving forlornly, interrupted the sandy, smooth, northward progression of the coast. The four had not seen another soul in the week's crossing of the timberland. They had become used to hearing only each other's voices and seeing only the familiar faces, so it was startling to see a group of fishermen ahead on the beach, perhaps a dozen of them, their tiny fishing boats dragged onto the sand. They were gathered around some object on the beach, perhaps a big fish they had landed, for it was well known that in this section of the country the fishermen often worked together, laying their nets in such a way that they encircled schools of fish, then brought their boats together to harvest the sea bounty.

"Let's take a look," Cal suggested, for it was clear that

the fishermen were excited by their catch, whatever it was. Even from a distance they could be seen jabbering away at each other in the local dialect. Their clothes were much different from those worn by the travelers. Instead of animal furs for warmth they wore coats made of the shiny inside-out skins of aquatic mammals to repel the water when they were at sea, and also against the frequent coastal rains and persistent drizzling fog that even now pervaded the air, clinging to everything and sending damp chills through the recent arrivals.

"It's none of our business," Endril warned. "Don't intrude unless you are asked. These folk are suspicious of strangers, and why not? How many invaders have first pushed their ships' prows onto this beach as prelude to terror, massacre, and ruination?"

"Well, that's true enough, but we came from inland, and it shows," Cal retorted, showing his youthful impatience, but he followed Endril's lead as the four started north, taking a path that would skirt the cluster of fisherfolk. They passed within a hundred yards of the group, who fell silent at the sight of outlanders (or really, inlanders) but soon returned to their agitated discussion among themselves. As they went by, the four each caught a glimpse of the carcass—it was a monstrous sea beast, with gaping toothy jaws and a rubbery skin, one immense dorsal fin sticking out at least seven feet sideways as the creature lay on its side.

"My goodness," Bith exclaimed, "what on earth is that?"

"Nothing on earth," Endril answered, "except in death. That is one of the creatures of the deep. It is said that fish like that—"

"That's no fish, that's a sea mammal, and a huge one, for only whales grow that large—" Cal interjected.

"You are wrong this time, Cal. That is a fish, though gargantuan. It is said that such fish live miles beneath the surface, only rising to pull an occasional boat beneath the water, for somewhere in the way below they have learned to crave the taste of human flesh."

When Hathor heard this he shuddered, and took his eyes off the gory sight. The fishermen had begun to slice up their apparent quarry, though the smell of the rotting carcass led Endril to speculate that they had not caught it at all but only found it washed ashore. They were almost out of sight of them when a lone member of the fishing party broke away and followed them, shouting in the queerly salty and colorful tongue of the region.

"Auslanders, strangers, wait ho!" he cried, running clumsily on the damp, loose sand.

"We had better talk to him. We don't know where their village is, and we don't want to trespass," Endril advised. So they all sat down in the gritty sand to wait for the one who had hailed them.

The fisherman had the weather-beaten look of someone who spends his life outdoors. His hair was permanently windswept, his face ruddy and lined, the skin around his eyes crinkly but the eyes themselves sharp and clear.

"How come ye to our shores? Know ye anything of yon beastie back there?" he asked jauntily, as if he feared them not a whit and knew that this was *his* land, *his* sea.

"We do not," Endril answered in measured terms, speaking for the group.

Then Hathor asked his question of the fisherman, because one never knows who might hold wisdom. "I want to know why you eat him."

The fisherman looked at him in startled surprise. "Because the sea is all that feeds us. D'ye think ye can grow corn on this sandy beach, then? Ye can't, but y' can salt enou' cod to trade with the farmers."

"Don't you think it hurts the fish?" Hathor asked, and the fisherman eyed him as one who is possessed.

"No, ye moon-drunk creature, the fishies is too dumb to feel it." Hathor shook his head as if he knew otherways, but said nothing.

"What be your destination?" the hardy seafarer asked,

and although his intent seemed harmless enough, Endril did not give a direct answer.

"We go north."

"North? There's bounteous much of nothing to the north. Why go ye north?"

"We have our reasons," said Cal, who didn't like to be challenged about anything, but Endril calmly reiterated his brief reply, adding: "We go north in peace."

"Peace? Good. Fine. Go in peace, then, but don't expect peace to greet you. The north is a harsh place, a drear place. Yon beastie came from the north, an' there be more and worse than it, both on land and at sea. Would you be wanting to rent a boat, then?"

Hathor grimaced, but to his relief Endril said no, they would be walking.

"Then ye had better start, for it's a mighty long walk to the north."

The seaman's suggestion was a veiled threat. All knew it, and Cal rebelled against it, puffing and snorting like a bull about to charge, but Endril coolly thanked the man for his advice and bid him farewell. As one they turned and started north up the beach, which curved gracefully in as the cliff diminished into the distance. For as far as they could see the cliff, beach, and water's edge formed a continuous set of parallel lines merging to a dark point on the far horizon. They could feel the penetrating gaze of the local man at their backs, but there was nowhere to avoid it on the narrow strip of sand between rock and sea. When, after an hour's hard march, they finally rested and looked back, he stood there yet, a mere speck but visible, his legs planted wide apart in the sailor's way, his stare still fixed upon them.

"He's a persistent son of a devil, isn't he?" Cal said disgustedly, for he would fain have shown the man the flat of his sword for his arrogance.

"Wrong again, Cal," Endril chided, "persistence is a good quality, perhaps the best. I have heard tell of a tribe to the east, across the Great Water, whose whole religion is based upon the words: 'Perseverance furthers.' " It was amazing how Endril could insult and educate them in the sentence.

"Besides," Bith asked, "how would you like it if four armed strangers showed up in your neighborhood—"

"Just as you found food," Hathor added morosely, for he was rummaging discouragedly through his rucksack for something to nibble, having survived his self-imposed penance of a week's worth of tree bark.

"I suppose you're right," Cal admitted. "Still, he seems awfully concerned about our progress. Where does he think we could go? We're trapped on this beach."

"Perhaps he expects to see boats land to meet us. Remember, when danger comes in these parts, it almost always comes from the sea."

"Let's move on," Hathor suggested, but Bith complained that they had only just stopped, so Hathor stomped off by himself toward the sea, hoping to find some edible seaweed or something, anything to relieve the gnawing hunger he felt. Even though the prevailing wind came out of the frozen north, and would be in their faces for the duration of their journey, Hathor swore to himself that he could scent the oily tons of fish flesh lying back there on the beach. Trolls, whose sense of smell is renowned, are said to be able to sniff out meat from great distances, but the gusty sea breeze should have prevented his catching any whiff of the decaying remains. *It must be in my weak brain*, Hathor decided, for he felt enfeebled by lack of food and lack of will, the will to resist the enticements of flesh-eating. And though he was a troll not a man, the saying of antiquity would apply to him equally, if only he knew it: "The strong man is he who overcomes himself."

The seaweed rooted up from the ocean floor or ripped from the skerries and tossed up onshore was tough and shiny and thoroughly indigestible, but it was softer than tree bark and Hathor nibbled unenthusiastically on it until he remembered that he still had three apples in a pocket of his greatcoat—he had searched only his carry-sack before.

With private joy he munched contentedly on one of the juicy fruits, not minding a bit the sandy grit that clung to it, not noticing the salty tang of the wind that blew the sand on it or the rumble from his protesting belly. When hailed by his comrades Hathor came slowly, chewing the last of the apple deliberately and swallowing the seeds whole as if he hoped they would sprout in his stomach, grow and nourish him from within.

Up ahead the cliff-bound shoreline curved inward for one of the few spots on the lengthy coast, creating a shallow bay, now at low tide a mudflat. Across the cove they could see the opposite outward curve where the straight northward progression of the cliff resumed. Had they not just rested they might have camped here for the night, and it was a likely spot for habitation, human or otherwise, but they saw no cooking smoke or trails or refuse or any other signs of life.

"Let's walk across the flats," Cal suggested. "It'll save us an hour at least."

"I don't like it," Endril warned. "We'd be awfully exposed out there. Anyone could see us from miles away. We'd be better off to hug the shore and work our way around."

"Anyone up on the cliffs can see us anyway," Cal insisted, and Bith complained she had sore feet and that the mud might feel good on them, and Hathor grumbled that the journey was long enough as is without prolonging it more, so Endril relented and they started across the mudflats. Endril removed his delicate, pointed shoes and Bith too went barefoot.

The mud bubbled and sank beneath them, sucking at their feet with each step, but they made good progress by having Hathor lead and everyone else follow in his wide footsteps. They were two thirds of the way across the muddy downs when a faint white line sprang up on the eastern horizon separating sea and sky, as if a tautly stretched rope were strung quivering across the mouth of the sound. All four of them noticed immediately this change in the constant wide-flung panorama of the Sea of Storms. This rope illusion twirled and danced and grew at the edge of vision, while under their feet the mud thrummed and vibrated.

"What is it, Endril?" Bith wanted to know.

"If it's what I think—yes—the tide is rushing in like a river! It must be a quirk of this shallow bay. May the gods help us!" There was no mistaking the panic in his voice, yet Endril remained in place as if the mud had clasped his feet. The others too were momentarily stunned by the far-off rumbling, as the rolling breakers, now clearly outlined against the sky, came onrushing at them, swelling and roaring.

"Don't you know a spell that might—"

"Spell? Are you mad? You think mere magic can work against the ceaseless strength of water? Even the gods could not hold back such a force. I know only one word for this—RUN!"

At that the four tore off for the far northern shore, running pell-mell and headlong in their fright. Hathor lost a boot and insisted on going back for it, which cost him precious seconds, but he knew that he could not survive a long trek without both boots, so he risked his life now to preserve it later. He was a hundred yards behind the others and a quarter mile from the high-water mark when the flowing tide overtook them, knocking them all down into the surf. They were swept forward head over heels up the narrowing channel cut by the tidal path.

Cal's sword dragged him under repeatedly until he got hold of it. Hathor's boots likewise hindered his efforts to stay afloat, and he was not a natural swimmer, but there was no real thought of swimming in this deluge, which bounced them off the channel walls like plumb-bobbins. Bith came up once and saw the mouth of the bay, a gap receding in the distance. Lighter than the others she floated easier on the spumy crest of the surge, but being feathery she tumbled more and easier, and the shifting chopping flux kept forcing her under. Her hair weighted down her head too, and she was in danger of being sucked under altogether when the inflow finally began to diminish.

"Try for the banks," Endril spluttered. No one could hear him above the water's tumult, but all had the same idea and eventually each of them was able to haul themselves out of the lessening swell, which by now was two miles inland from the bay and up into the confluence of a usually down-flowing river. Where sweet water met salt water the two swirled together and the advancing tide lost momentum in a series of dizzying whirlpools. After spinning free from these treacherous vortexes the four bedraggled adventurers clambered up the shallow bank, and lay on their stomachs, all of them, coughing and spitting water and gasping for lungfuls of precious air.

Endril seemed the least battered—he rounded them up and started a fire with that nifty little trick of his for producing such things out of thin air. Their possessions were thoroughly soaked, and their bodies were bruised from the buffeting of the waves, but they were alive.

"What sort of spell could have caused that?" Cal wondered when they were all huddled naked under soggy blankets round a satisfactory blaze while their clothes dried.

"No spell at all, as I told you out there when we first saw it. You look too much for the supernatural. Often the world itself, nature, is more magical than the greatest magician. Is it magic that in spring the distant sun makes hidden seeds sprout in rock-hard ground frozen all winter? Is it magic that you are fast with your sword or that Hathor is strong? Take a long shallow sloping bay, a confluence of flow and wind and moon's pull, and you have the makings of a running tide such as the one that caught us."

"The Claviger—" Bith spoke from beneath her protective covering, her silvery eyes brighter than the bright fire's flame reflecting in them.

"Eh?" Endril, caught off-guard, could only manage a surprised grunt. The next instant he recovered enough to ask sharply: "How do you know of him?"

"The Keeper of the Keys,
Yes it is he who doth please,
He who unlocks the Mysteries—"

Bith sang—Bith and not Bith, someone, something else, a voice that quavered and wavered, came and went. Bith had been possessed by some spirit or sprite. She swayed before the fire like a penitent, her eyes now rolled upward showing white.

Endril motioned for the others to remain still. He then proceeded to question the invader in Bith's body. "Do you bring a message from the Claviger? What are your intentions?"

"Does Vili have anything to do with this?" Cal hissed to Endril, but the intensely concentrating elf ignored him. The wraith within Bith spoke again, in that peculiar singsongy voice that was not Bith's own.

"Look to your oxen,
Look to your sheaves,
Look to the drowsy hum of bees,
All are rewards from the Keeper of Keys—"

"Must be a rhyming relative of yours—" Cal joked in a whisper, for he was still not captivated like the others by the sense-stealing mood of the possession.

"Hush!" was all Endril replied before the voice of the apparition again issued from the mouth of Bith.

"The Keeper has made you protectors of earth,
Of mountain and valley and fjord and firth,

Of plants and fish and all things growing,
Dogs baying, mules braying, and cattle lowing.
Turn back on your primitive savage ways
These are new and gentle days."

"Strange words to recite to a soldier," Cal responded,
but the voice went on, the song continued:

"The flesh-eaters rage and tear and gore
When blood runs they cry more, more, more!
The Keeper knows that for all to prosper
Plant-eater, meat-eater, and man the master
Must harmonize or face disaster.
One there is who seeks to return
To the blood lust of those who ravage and burn.
Stop him, Good Hathor—"

The three listeners were startled to hear one of their party addressed directly by the shadowy voice—"Stop him—
stop him—stop him . . ." The voice trailed away like the
lingering echo of an echo, like a cloud dissolving into blue
sky, and Bith collapsed as if she were felled by a blow from
Hathor's axe.

Of course she knew nothing of what she had uttered, and
had to be told the whole story by Cal, while Endril mused
quietly on the episode and Hathor, amazed that he should
be named, sat in a stupefied silence.

"There can no longer be any doubt that Hathor's quest
is our own. When he finds out why he is tormented by
his appetite for flesh, we will find the object of our long
march," Endril declared.

"What in Freya's Folly has that got to do with the Mistwall, the Dark Lord, or anything else we've battled before?"
Bith asked, and Cal stated bluntly:

"You'll never see me giving up a good roast for a leaf,
fruit, or root. A soldier must needs have meat for strength
and courage." Cal found the whole prospect unsettling.

"No one is asking you to do so, Cal," said Endril, but soon the two were engaged in a roaring argy-bargy over the point. Hathor, feeling justly honored to have been chosen for such an important role, sat quietly aside and listened. Bith was still weak from the possession and also said nothing while the lively discussion raged. Finally she could restrain herself no longer.

"Who is the Claviger?" she asked Endril, but surprisingly, it was Hathor who answered.

"The Keeper of Keys," he said.

"We heard that," Cal said impatiently. "Keys to what?"

"Everything."

"Everything? What do you mean?"

"Claviger is greatest of gods."

"What! Greater than Freya? Greater than mighty Thor himself?" Cal, simple loyal soldier that he was, was shocked to hear his pantheon being belittled, or so it seemed to him. "Why haven't I heard of him before?"

"Claviger came before your gods," was Hathor's answer. "Tell him, Endril."

All looked to Endril. The elf settled slowly back against the rock that propped him up. He reached into his drying vest and pulled a long straight-stemmed clay pipe from it, but put nothing in it, merely clenching it once or twice between his teeth, then holding it comfortably with one hand as he began his story.

"Elves and trolls have their own gods, but they share one deity—the Claviger, the Keeper of the Keys as we have heard him called tonight, also known as He Who Came Before."

"Before what?" Cal asked.

"Before All. Before the Earth and Sky were separated. Before men and animals were born. When everything rested in a state of sameness, without form or feeling, a grey mass of nothing, Claviger was there. It was he who struck the flint that showered the sparks of life in all its wondrous forms."

"Why made he some this way and some that?" Hathor

strained for words to convey his cloudy thoughts, for though he knew the story it was vague in his rusty brain.

"He has many Keys, has the Keeper, and he uses them all."

"But why make some only to be consumed by others? It serves no purpose," sturdy, practical-minded Cal pointed out.

"Who are we to say what is the Keeper's ken? And besides, everything is consumed by everything else. Naught remains the same. Even these great boulders along the shore of this inlet will be eaten away unto pebbles by the gentle but relentless water could we sit here long enough to witness it."

"Which we can't," Cal said, still grousing over the turn of events.

"It is rare, so very rare, to receive a missive from the Claviger. We should all consider ourselves fortunate to have heard from him, and do our utmost to obey his command—"

"But he gave none," Cal objected. "Nothing specific. Nothing you could pass down a line of command and say 'Do this!' or 'Do that!' to a company of troops. Only vague, veiled threats and a warning. Not even a name—"

"Hathor." With a single growl, Hathor reminded them of his importance to the story.

"No, you big tree-chopper, not you, I mean the name of our nameless, faceless adversary. At least sometimes Vili helps us. This Claviger seems only to pontificate while scaring the soul out of princesses—"

"I wasn't scared," Bith protested. "I didn't even know what happened."

"Well, inhabiting them, then."

"I want you to show respect for the Claviger," Endril said quietly, but there was a quality of seriousness in the elf's voice, and a certain uprightness and stiff-neckedness in his tall posture that gave Cal pause.

"Me too," Hathor grunted, with feeling.

"Alright then," Cal assented. "But I ask as Bith did,

what does this have to do with the Mistwall and our present sojourn?"

"We know now to guard Hathor—he is somehow the key—"

"Key, keys, Keeper! It's all too much for me. Do we continue north?" he asked bluntly.

"We do," Endril answered.

"That's good enough for me," said Cal, and he pulled his crude covering over him to sleep a soldier's sleep.

Endril tamped his still-unfilled pipe against a nearby fallen log. Without a word he too curled into a position of rest. Hathor, already drowsy from so much talking, soon filled the air with his snores, and Bith, exhausted by her ordeal in the water, passed into a rejuvenating slumber. Soon the campfire waned and burnt itself out, and the four lay resting where the tide had flung them like so much living flotsam. The moon rose and flooded the hollow with a silky light. They had come so far, and yet their journey had barely begun.

CHAPTER
6

The next morning they retraced the inlet to its source. The mudflat lay again exposed at low tide, a quiet, inviting, rippled brown surface. A few birds skittered after small crabs, or fluttered down to pluck for mussels between tidal pools left here and there at the end of seeping rills or behind sandbars. Otherwise the shoal was deserted.

This time they prudently avoided the open but treacherous flats and followed the curve of the bay 'til they came to a low ridge at its northern edge. When they climbed the ridge they spied on the other side the first human habitation they had seen in many days.

"Hooray!" Cal shouted. "I see a hornful of mead in my future!"

"Think you they serve such as that here? Salted fish and ale is what you're likely to get."

"My clothes are in shreds from yesterday. Do you think there's a seamstress in that whole village?" Bith wondered aloud.

In truth they did look a sight. Of course Hathor always attracted attention, but today his bearskin coat was muddied and matted and his red hair the same. They each had received scratches and bruises from the tumbling of the day before, and even sprightly Endril looked slightly bedraggled after ten days in the wilderness.

"We'll wash up and drink up and rest up a day or two here before going on," he said. A trail led down between the giant boulders of the shore ridge to the village, leading out onto the dead end of a cleared street where it ran up against the rise. Up ahead was a line of twenty or so buildings that comprised the village.

Cal collared the first person who came toward them, a rag merchant dragging a creaky cart piled high with odds and ends of torn and dirty cloth. The man had placed himself in the traces of the cart, which was meant to be pulled by an animal, either ox or horse, and was the beast of burden himself. Apparently he was leaving the hamlet and abandoning the dead-end street and was about to try to climb the hill trail with the cart in tow, though Cal couldn't imagine where he was going after that, or why. He seemed in a hurry, but Cal halted him anyway with an upraised arm.

"Ho there, rag-man. Be you of these parts?"

"Aye," came the surly response.

"We nearly drowned in that quick tide you have back there at the flats. How often does it do that?"

"What's that?" the townsman asked, edging away from Cal.

"You know," said Cal, "the sudden rush of water up the inlet, as if six hours' worth of intide happens all at once."

"Never seen that," the townsman answered abruptly, and turned away, yanking at the staves of his cart to hoist it over the first of many obstacles in his rocky path.

"Is he playing games with me?" Cal asked Endril out of the side of his mouth, but Endril pulled Cal away from the suspicious stranger and hustled him down the street, leaving the ragger to struggle with his impossible cargo.

"What did he mean he didn't know?" Cal ranted. "If that flood doesn't happen twice a day, then it must come with the moon cycle, or every seven years, or sometime!"

"Or else it was magic after all."

"Oh!" Cal sneered. "After all your talk about the natural magic of the world, now you admit that someone might have been practicing black arts on us."

"Yes," said Endril, but he wasn't thinking about yesterday's problems any longer. The four had entered the village. Along one side of the lone street was a single wharf. The village took advantage of the partial shelter offered by the jutting slip of rock that formed the northern edge of the mudflat bay. That recess where they had been swept away was too shallow for boats to enter, but here on the other side of the northern arm of the flats there was no beach, only a cove with a deep draught right up to the rocky shore. The villagers had built a wooden jetty out over the water for a dock.

On the other side of the street the grey, weathered houses of the village lined up in a row, each with its back to the hillside and its front facing the sea. Some of the houses had fenced walkways atop them as lookouts. All of them looked to be very old, and worn from years of beating salt spray and buffeting wind.

Above and to the right of the village, the group saw for the first time a manor house that had been hidden from view by a second hillock when they had spotted the town from the ridge. It almost seemed a separate entity from the village, as if it were too lofty proud to have anything to do with those common seaside shanties. Nestled into the hills and freshly painted white, it gleamed in the morning sun against a backdrop of green forest.

"What a fine house. Not a castle, but still grand," Bith breathed. "I wonder who lives there."

"We'll find out," said Cal, but then his face turned grim. "Why do you suppose that rag fellow was in such a hurry to leave this place?" he asked without addressing anyone. They found themselves alone on the street. A few coracles rode at anchor, tugging at their mooring lines, their sides scraping the dock melodically and halyards clanking against their masts rhythmically in the breeze. Except for the fleeing rag-man, they had seen no one.

"Perhaps we are so far north they have never seen trolls," Bith suggested, but Endril scoffed at the notion.

"Even where we are headed, in the land of the Wind-Websters, there are trolls. That is not the problem here, though humans always seem to have difficulty with any-one different from themselves. Something else is happen-ing here," was Endril's assessment of the situation. "Bith, what do you make of it? Do you sense anything strange in the air?"

Endril's question was so pointed that all of them tensed as if to heighten their senses, but Bith shrugged and said nothing.

"There's someone, of sorts," Cal noted. Down the street in front of the largest building in the village (which might or might not be an inn, as there was no sign out front nor any indication of stables or a hostelry), two children dressed in what could have been scraps fallen from the rag-man's wag-on were playing at a peg and board game. They entertained themselves silently and solemnly, without childish laughter and excitement, ignoring the strangers as if the toy were a life or death struggle.

"Devil and the tailor," Bith said, but Cal called it "fox and geese," and Hathor knew it by another name altogether. The two young players did not even look up as the four surrounded them, a curious audience to a curious contest. Finally one of them won by "jumping over" the last row of the other's defensive pegs. Somberly, ceremoniously, and formally the two combatants nodded to each other, one picked up the board and the other pocketed the pegs and they both disappeared soundlessly around the corner of the building before the amazed travelers could utter a word.

"We ought to question them. I'll go after them," Cal suggested when they had recovered from their momentary shock.

"You won't get anything from those two. They were deaf-mutes, couldn't you see that?" Bith said.

"Or playing deaf and dumb, more likely," Cal replied, chafing at Bith's tone.

They were spared further bickering by a tremendous shout that arose from within the building, bursting so suddenly and forcefully into the lengthy silence that Cal jumped back and half drew his sword and Hathor's hand instinctively went to the handle of his axe. The cheer sustained itself for a few seconds, then fell off and gave way again to the soothing rhythmic sounds of sea and wind.

"Everyone in the village must be inside, to make such a racket," said Cal.

"What is it all about?" Hathor asked nervously, because he didn't like things to be so uncertain and mysterious.

"Let's find out," said Endril, and striding to the door, he opened it and walked in, leaving it open, which was just as well for him, because in a few seconds there was a stir and a rumble and suddenly Endril came flying out the door on his backside, not magic-flying but flung by angry villagers who came to the door, examined rugged Hathor and the other motley adventurers, and threw the door shut on them with a crash.

Endril dusted himself off casually. "Local politics," he said smugly, but as none of his fellows had ever seem him handled thus, they kept their distance and did not answer.

"What do we do now?" Hathor, still befuddled, wanted to know.

"I say we wander on up to the manor house. Perhaps we'll receive more favorable treatment there," Endril suggested.

"Yes, that's more to my liking too," Bith echoed.

Hathor went along, although he suspected that he'd end up in the barn as he had before when they'd visited other wealthy land-vested humes. Sometimes the kept hounds ate better than he did at these stopovers. Unlike villagers, who were usually only fearful and amazed to see trolls, the petty barons and clan chiefs who owned manorial homes and land were often hostile and arrogant toward him, though from what Hathor could see of their lives they were no different from him, except perhaps they smelled less and dressed cleaner, but what was that to Hathor? Nothing. As the four of them walked up the path into the cool forest again, Hathor made a decision.

"I will not go in," he said. The others knew immediately what he meant. Endril too had received rudeness at the hands of these local lords, who often combined the worst qualities of villagers, their small-mindedness and suspicious natures, with the least attractive of a ruler's ways: imperiousness, haughtiness, and a false sense of their own power and importance.

"Oh, Hathor." Bith stamped a foot impatiently, for she imagined the house to be a palace of luxury and was tired of sleeping on rocks and grass or sand as they had for days and days.

"I will not," Hathor repeated, and to show his intent he broke off the trail and sat down. Endril and Bith joined him, but Cal remained standing on the path. They were less than a quarter mile from the house, which was again in sight after having disappeared into the greenery as they climbed toward it. The forest before it had been cleared away, which was why it was visible at all from the shore. In place of underbrush a fine green lawn had been planted, which sloped away from the frontage to a cliff above the Sea of Storms. Statuary lined the sides of the great rolling plot at intervals, and behind the statuary the forest picked up again solidly on both sides, so that this unusual swatch of grass stood out vibrantly.

"The views from the front bartizan there must be spectacular," Cal commented. "No one could attack you from the front with that cleared field and cliff before you. And behind, a steep hillside. The perfect fortification."

"What about this broad path we climb?" Endril jibed.

"Ah, but you have the villagers and their village at the

bottom of the hill as a first defense against enemies from land or sea."

"What if the villagers *are* the enemy?" Endril asked enigmatically, but Bith brought the two of them back to the main point.

"Won't you convince good Hathor to come with us?" she pleaded, but it was no use. The stolid troll was determined. He had suffered enough humiliation, there was no reason to bring more down on his head. The forest floor was good enough for him, the barn no better.

"I wait for you here," was the most he would say. At last they persuaded the recalcitrant troll to follow behind, and *if* the manor holder was a good man, and *if* he was invited, for Hathor to come in.

"Why should he see us?" Cal asked no one in particular, but Bith answered him quickly.

"Good nobles always want to hear the news of the world. Travelers are honored—"

"Distinguished travelers—yes. But a scruffy lot like ourselves, begging your princess's pardon, are we likely to get any better reception than Hathor fears?"

"Hathor fears nothing—" the troll bespoke for himself, but Endril broke in.

"I think we might be better received than in ordinary times. Something extraordinary is going on here."

"You said that before. Have you any more details now?" Cal pressed him.

"The villagers threw me out as a stranger, without even bothering to ask which side I was on. Obviously this is not a skirmish of some larger conflict, but a local strife. Not often, but every now and again one hears of brave groups of men who rise up against cruel lords, and o'erthrow them."

"And which side would you have us on?" Cal wondered, for he was confused. As a squire, his loyalty had been unquestioned and unquestionable—for his lord's sake and safety he would have slaughtered any riffraff who rose against him. But now, it seemed, he must judge for himself right and wrong, and place his loyalties on that basis. And this situation was not at all clear. "If we are supporters of the right, why would we offer our services to a local tyrant?"

"We do not go to work for the man, only to seek refuge and shelter for a night. This is not our fight. But who knows what might happen? And further, after the events of the past few days, who is to say what might be in our path?"

This left Cal feeling only more perplexed than before. He turned to face the shining white citadel, which was truly a splendid edifice, though constructed of wood rather than stone. Most of the castles Cal had seen before rose out of bedrock. This was more like a great hall, boxy and straight-sided, set straight into the forest ground, but still possessing defensive bartizans and turrets across its long front, though there was no moat or fosse around it, nor a keep atop it. Like a giant replica of the houses in the village, this one had a rooftop walkway rimmed by a low fence, affording the best views of the harbor and the sea beyond.

"Let's go then," Cal said, and the others rose from their resting spots.

Hathor needn't have worried, they discovered, for the lord was delighted to have visitors, once he quelled the racket from his dozen vicious guard dogs, which went slightly berserk when they caught wind of Hathor. Though the interior courtyard was strongly guarded by heavyset soldiers with maces and coulter-knives on spears, the main door had been thrown open in anticipation of their arrival, and the lord of the manor stood in the doorway, filled the doorway, to greet them. Though smaller than Hathor, he was huge for a human, perhaps six and a half feet tall, with reddish-blond hair almost Hathor's color but much longer, curling down past his shoulders in the back, and a full beard the same shade of red. He wore a hefty skin-coat not unlike Hathor's but clean and shiny, with studs and buckles that dressed it up, and a horned helmet covered in the same skin to match, so that the effect was regal and imposing, entirely different from Hathor's shabby appearance.

"Obviously we were spotted from above, and deemed to be no threat," Cal whispered to Bith as they approached the entrance gate, a single heavy wooden door with iron bands running across its entire outer surface top to bottom.

Beating the hounds with the butt end of a nasty-looking whip, he drove them back inside the container, then gestured in welcome to all of them, not excluding Hathor. In fact the lord was unusually friendly toward the troll, introducing himself to Hathor first.

"Welcome to Steadfast-by-Sea. I welcome you. My ancestors welcome you. And my unborn sons the rulers of this place evermore welcome you."

From within now Cal gave the place a quick survey, as he had been trained to do. He could see that the house was not solid, rather instead a rectangle with an inside court open to the sky, where soldiers drilled and lounged, and weapons were stacked. A well at the center of the dusty bare yard provided fresh water, the one essential to surviving a siege, Cal noted. In a protracted siege, you could always make some few provisions stretch many weeks, but without water, you perished, he mused, but then the lord was giving his name and Cal turned his attention back to the man.

"I am Threnod, sometimes known as Threnod the Shieldor, Steadfast-by-Sea's sole rightful heir and owner. And who might you be?"

Endril made a round of introductions. Threnod the Shieldor paid particular attention to the two non-humans of the four, which upset Bith just a little, as she was used to getting the most attention in such situations.

"So big and strong you are, a good smithy you would make," Threnod said approvingly of Hathor's trollish muscles. "And how tall and handsome is your kind," he complimented Endril, who ignored such flattery for what it was. Endril was, like Cal, examining the interior courtyard in detail. Threnod asked him about it.

"Have you not seen fortifications such as ours before?"

"Aye. But a long time ago, and across the Sea of Storms."

"My ancestors, perhaps."

"Perhaps."

"What brings you to Steadfast-by-Sea?" He and Endril were like chess players or swordsmen, feeling each other out with questions.

"We are travelers, following the coast north. We wish only a night's lodging and a meal if thou canst spare it." The elf fell unconsciously into the old formal way of speaking when addressing Threnod, as if he were remembering an earlier encounter sometime in the dim past.

"Of course, of course. But you were saying, north to—?" the immense Lord Threnod tried Endril, but the elf skirted the question.

"North."

"You came through town just now?"

"We did."

"Saw you anyone?"

"All at a meeting. I saw them briefly." Cal chuckled at the memory of Endril flying out feet first, but the cool, tense dialogue between Endril and Lord Threnod continued.

"Yes. They are meeting. They hate me, you know."

"Yes." Endril's answer surprised his companions. Had he learned more in his few seconds inside the village meetinghouse than he let on?

"The wretches. They should think what their lives were like before I came. But come, come, let us dine in the Hall of Shields, and talk of heroes and valiant deeds, not traitors and shame."

"I like the sound of that," Cal rang out, for he was quickly growing to admire this upright warrior-lord. He liked the man's style. They followed Threnod through a columned anteroom into the Hall of Shields, where a marvelous spectacle awaited them. All four walls of the room were covered with shields of all shapes and sizes, some circular, some square, some cloth-covered and some forged, some draped in chain mail like Cal's ailette. Markings and symbols were blazoned on their escutcheons, armorial insignia of crosses and circles and painted animals and birds, gryllus and griffons, lions and eagles, each representing a clan or a tribe or an army or its leader. Some of the defensive armor pieces were battered and cracked, some pierced and stove in, others barely scratched. On the far wall above the collection, which vibrated with the fading echoes of so many battles and so much strife, was a banner that proclaimed:

THESE DIED PROUD

"All of these are from dead men?" Bith asked Cal, and Cal nodded solemnly, thinking of the many glorious swings of the sword, the stands and heroic combats these shields represented.

The light in the Hall of Shields labored down through the smoke and pale from high slit windows in dim shafts, illuminating some shields and leaving others in gloomy obscurity. Interspersed among the row upon row of shields, which even covered the ceiling, were other gruesome trophies of war, spears and flags, weapons of lethal design, but it was the uniform hanging of the aegis, like a ghost army on display, that gave the Hall of Shields its name and its noble, heroic resonance.

"Come, sit," Threnod commanded, and to waiting servants he shouted: "Bring ale by the flagon, nay by the firkin! Hurry!"

The substantial table was carved in the pointed oval shape of a boat deck, and the chairs were iron-banded empty oak ale casks. Lord Threnod sat on an oversize keg himself, while his guests took their places beneath the savage display. The solemn roomful of war memories seemed an unlikely place to eat, but Lord Threnod had ordered a meal and it soon came—heaping platters of meat and fish, and tankards of nut-brown ale. The servingmen were burly fellows like their lord. One of the largest set a plateful of bony chops before

Hathor, then stood back and crossed his arms in anticipation of watching Hathor chomp into it, for it was well known that cracking bones was a trollish delight. When Hathor only looked revulsed and pushed the pile of steaming meat away from him, the servingman looked at his lord in dismay.

"Our food does not please you, Big One?" Lord Threnod inquired in a loud, unpleasant voice.

"Our companion eats no meat," Endril explained for the tongue-tied troll.

This amused Lord Threnod greatly. He laughed so hard he choked and had to quaff a quart of ale in one gulp to constrain himself. "A troll who chews his cud like an ox. It's perfect. Who could have known? What punishment!"

"To what does he refer?" Bith asked Endril, but the elf was as mystified as she; Lord Threnod apparently knew who they were, and even had plans for them. This was dangerous.

"Do you play the crwth?" Lord Threnod asked Endril suddenly. Endril admitted that he had mastered it, though he allowed that he did not carry one with him.

"I have one." Lord Threnod snapped his fingers imperiously. A loathsome minion ran to fetch the shallow-bodied string instrument, much like a harp, that could be bowed or plucked by musicians such as Endril.

"I like a bit of song with my drappy." He leered at Endril while hoisting another mug of ale toward his greasy lips.

"I'm not in the mood for playing," Endril said. Lord Threnod slammed his tankard down on the planks of the table so hard it shattered, spraying foamy suds of ale and shards of pottery over the platters of food. The oversize handle remained in his clenched hand like a threat.

"Play!" he ordered.

"Appease him, we're outnumbered," Cal whispered to the recalcitrant elf, for numerous of the lord's guards had crowded into the Hall of Shields for a look at the troll, the elf, the fair-skinned princess, and the young warrior, but Endril refused again.

"If it please, your lordship, I too can play the crwth," Bith offered, to the surprise of her companions, who had never heard this talent displayed by their erstwhile princess.

The servingman returned at that moment, and after a moment's hesitation Lord Threnod nodded to him to hand the delicate instrument to Bith.

Then, without trickery or magic, without lulling them to sleep or drugging them, Bith entranced her audience with melody, with the beauty of her quavering voice and the play of her dancing fingers across the quivering strings. She sang a ballad of tragic love, the story of the noble Osric and his love for the maiden Eanfled:

"Once on the fine green fields of Wold
Across the great blue River Tyne
Young Osric, fearless, brave, and bold
Did for fair sweet Eanfled pine.

"The river kept them from each other
The river and the curse of war
When every man fought with his brother,
Bloody battles, fierce and sore.

"The two young lovers pledged a meeting
Within the idle forest deep,
Eanfled's father Eanred found them
In each other's arms asleep.

"Wicked Eanred felled Osric with one stroke,
Smote him before he could stand and fight.
Cried his daughter when she awoke:
'You've killed the sun, now there is only night.'

"Before the hour of e'entide vespers
Eanfled into the River Tyne had leapt.
The chattering wind the story whispers
That in each other's arms again the lovers slept."

Bith finished her singing and strummed the last few mournful chords on the crwth. A single large tear ran from the corner of Lord Threnod's right eye down his florid cheek. He sighed loudly and deeply.

"Magnificent music, young woman. It is a pity we have to treat you so poorly."

"What do you mean?" Bith asked warily, and the other three guests of the savage lord became alert.

"Seize them!" Lord Threnod commanded, and almost before they could rise the four were surrounded by soldiers pouring into the room from all sides. The four fighters took up their box defense, each with a shoulder to the next in a tight formation, all facing out; but the situation looked bleak.

"We desire the troll alive. The others you may do with what you will," the lord decreed. Hathor groaned silently that he had again drawn his comrades into danger. But then there was no time to think or groan, only to fend and rend, crash and mash, strike and reel and turn and churn, for he was Hathor the Troll, great axe-wielder in the Hall of Shields, fighting for his life.

At first the battle went their way, as the soldiers, obeying Lord Threnod's orders, repeatedly attacked Bith, Cal, and Endril, leaving Hathor free to ply his axe trade with deadly effect. After he had split open the skulls of six of Lord Threnod's private guard, a net-caster managed to drop his snare over the incensed troll, and as he struggled to free himself, Hathor received a deep stab wound to the thigh and a blow on the head that would have killed a human, but only stunned Hathor into submission.

Losing contact with the downed Hathor, the other three drew up into a triangle and fought their way out of the Hall of Shields by pure force of will. Once in the open interior courtyard they were able to maneuver into a defensible position in the center of the space, but as more and more of the lord's men were summoned, they were increasingly pressured.

"Did you spy a postern?" Cal shouted over the battle's hue and cry, hoping the elf had seen a back door or tunnel that he had missed in his survey of the grounds earlier.

Endril, fencing with two broadswordsmen and keeping his limbs only by prodigious leaps under the clumsy but lethal swipes of the slower, heavier weapons, could only grunt in the negative as he dodged another sword swing. He lunged forward with his rapier at the hairy belly of his foe, gashing the man's rib cage but not delivering a fatal blow, the one weakness of the thin-bladed sword he favored.

"Make for the gate!" he urged Bith and Cal, but it was hopeless, the lord had posted his heaviest guard at the main entrance. Just when it looked like they would have to lay down their arms and surrender to an uncertain future, there was a commotion at the main gate. It bulged inward once, twice, and suddenly burst into wicked splinters flying inward at the guard. A mob of enraged townspeople, hearing the sounds of combat coming from the grand hall of Steadfast-by-Sea, had massed and charged the hill, reaching the gate with a battering ram while the guards were distracted by the fight within.

Poorly armed with sticks and staves, and spar poles and gaffs from their boats, they were quickly put on the defensive by Lord Threnod's disciplined house guard. Within a few minutes they were turned out again, but Bith, Cal, and Endril had escaped with them.

Not content to leave it at that, Lord Threnod's soldiers, their blood gorge up and their battle fever fierce, chased the unruly but overmatched, fleeing mob down the hill toward town. Torches were lit and homes burned. The battle took on the appearance of a massacre as women and children, cowering in their homes, were dragged into the street and butchered. The three remaining companions fought at the head of the townsfolk, organizing them and urging them to stand and fight rather than be slaughtered at heel, but against the fury of the troops they were virtually helpless. The remaining people of the town were swept along with

Bith, Cal, and Endril to the edge of the dock. It was a total defeat—they were being driven from their homes, their backs to the water. They could either fight and die or drown.

"Take to the boats," Cal yelled, and the sea villagers made a halfhearted effort to comply, but it was clear that even there the arrows and spears of the troops would reach them before they could make headway to sea. It had all happened so fast—a few minutes before they had boldly assaulted their oppressor and now his henchmen threatened to obliterate them all.

"Bith! Can't you do anything?" Cal pleaded, and indeed, the princess had been imagining what sort of spell might be useful, but nothing had come to her.

Hearing the desperation in his voice, Bith furrowed her brow and thought even harder. Suddenly it came to her. In the midst of the furious losing battle, she knelt behind a pier piling and clutched her purple stone, while chanting these words:

"Whirl and wither, storm and dither,
Whip up white-spray, sea to swell.
Make the ocean roll and blither
As I cast this WIND-RISE spell."

The day, which had been mildly grey, took on a sudden gloomy cast. As if from nowhere, clouds assembled along the horizon, rushing toward shore, blackening the sky and churning the ocean into turbulent foam as they came.

The soldiers, momentarily frightened by this unlikely specter, eased up their attack long enough for the towns-people to assist their young, elderly, and womenfolk into the boats and to cast off, the three companions scrambling into the last boat of a small fleet. The howling wind filled their sails and tore at the riggings as it carried them beyond the reach of the shore, over the breakers, and into the boiling open waters of the Sea of Storms.

From the tiny window of a cell, high beneath the toothy merlons that topped the crenellated parapets of Steadfast-by-Sea, Hathor watched sadly as his only friends in the world were swept away by a black storm. No one could survive such a tempest. He would never see them again. And what was his fate at the hands of Lord Threnod? Who was the buyer who had expressed interest in him before he had even arrived at Steadfast-by-Sea? Alone in the world, Hathor grieved for his friends, for himself, and for the village that lay in smoldering devastation below.

CHAPTER
7

"Get up, you ugly son of the unnatural." A bucket of cold water heaved through the cell door jarred Hathor from uneasy sleep just before dawn. He sputtered and roared, and charged the iron bars of the cage, but to no avail, they were driven deep into foot-square beams in the ceiling and floor.

"Back, you ungodly miscreant!" It was Lord Threnod himself, come to torment his prisoner.

"Did the rats keep you awake? They must work quite hard to climb all the way up here. They find the cellar dungeons much more leisurely—but that would be too homelike for you, you cousin of the worm! Better you teeter-totter up here in this high cell."

In truth Hathor did not enjoy being so far from the warm ground, and he disliked immensely the slight shaking of the tower in the breeze. Seeing this, Lord Threnod bounced his massive weight off the floor once or twice for effect. The parapet swayed ever so slightly, but Hathor grimaced and his stomach went queasy on him.

"Ha!" Threnod the Shieldor laughed, satisfying his own cruelty. "Ha!—the trembling bothers you. Think how it might have been had you escaped with your fellows. You'd be as green as that sea out there."

What Lord Threnod said was true, but it did not diminish the aching Hathor felt in his heart when he thought of his charge, Bith the Princess, and his good friends Cal the Squire and Endril the Elf—but wait—his captor had said "escaped"! Was it possible they had weathered the storm? The plodding troll could figure out no clever way to ask Lord Threnod, so he simply stated the question directly.

"Did they live?"

Lord Threnod shrugged his shoulders indifferently. "They survived our soldiers' spears and their arrows, which we like to call 'messengers of death.' Whether they outrode the sudden storm, I cannot say. We'll search the coast for washed-up bodies"—Lord Threnod brightened—"and I'll bring their bloated, battered bodies for your inspection, yes."

Hathor groaned at the grisly image. "What of me?" he asked.

"You? My prize? My pot of gold? Your purchaser arrives tomorrow. He has a surprise fate in store for you. Yes, we have had many a good laugh over this one, I daresay. Even now as I think of it—ha!" Lord Threnod chuckled and chortled, and the tower shook again under his quaking bulk. "But I swore I would not give away the secret—you must wait—that's it, you must wait!" With that Lord Threnod jounced from the room, leaving the unhappy troll clutching the bars of his cell in anguish and fear. The room was in no danger of toppling from its perch, but to Hathor each wisp of breeze seemed to shake it.

He stared out of the slit window at the narrow strip of sea he was able to observe. Now becalmed, the waters gave no sign of the turbulence of yesterday's sudden storm. A faint flicker of hope arose in Hathor's groggy brain: perhaps that was one of Bith's magic spells, come to rescue them. But then he shook his massive head and ground his teeth. *No, you cannot command the sea and wind, they command you.*

And even if it was her magic, so many times she did too little or too much, and caused worse disasters for the ones she meant to help. *And the sea, the sea,* Hathor thought dismally. Hathor was an earth creature. To him the oceans were a living monster, huge and threatening. He would even prefer this eagle's nest prison cell to the deck of a rolling ship in a storm.

His cell had one interesting feature: slit holes had been cut in the beam planking so that defending archers and spearmen could shoot straight down. Hathor discovered them almost right away, for they were most noticeable; they provided an unusual view, and Hathor avoided them as they made him dizzy. There were a half dozen of them at intervals in two rows of three, so that as many as six men could shoot at once.

"Messengers of death." Hathor remembered Lord Threnod's joking remark. What was he to do? Escape was impossible. Resigning himself to his fate, Hathor decided to go back to sleep. He had just settled into a comfortable snooze when he was again brutally riven awake by the sound of his cell door crashing open.

"Come with me!" Lord Threnod again appeared before him, breathing hard and sweating from the climb.

He could almost be one of mine, Hathor thought but he wisely (for a troll) kept his tongue.

"My soldiers want a bit of sport before they have to give you up."

Because he was being sold, Hathor knew that Lord Threnod had to keep him in reasonable shape to get the best price. Even a dull-witted troll likes to get a good bargain at market price. So he didn't imagine that he'd have to fight, or that he'd suffer torture; after all, his new owner was arriving tomorrow, there would be no time for wounds to heal.

"My new owner," Hathor sighed to himself as three of Lord Threnod's guards surrounded him. One slipped a dog collar on him, a studded leather band fastened to a metal chain of forged links. He was led by the neck down the passageway to the interior stairwell of the wooden castle. How easily he was letting himself slip into the role of the slave. *No,* he resolved, *I must resist, I must not become any man's vassal.*

"Where do we go?" he asked, yanking on the chain with which the lead guard conducted him.

"We're going to stuff you like a greylag goose. Fatten you up for the butcher's block—oh! I made another joke on you!" Lord Threnod gasped between rolling fits of raucous, hard-edged laughter.

Hathor could easily imagine himself as a meal for others more bloodthirsty than his former self. He had seen gorier pots aboiling, and witnessed terrible troll initiation sessions where the bloodiest raw warm organs were consumed as part of ritual entry into trollhood. But it seemed an awful lot of trouble for just a single meal for anyone, troll or hume. At least he would finally meet his tormentor, who had hurled foedingbats and slizards, a dragon, torrents of water, and who knows what all else against him.

Why me? Hathor wondered silently, asking the ages-old question of one wronged without reason.

For now he could worry only about the chafing collar around his neck, and about staying alive for the day, the moment. The future was a dark road of loneliness without his friends who had been borne away to an uncertain fate. Ahead of him walked swaggering, arrogant Lord Threnod, who was not a true lord, Hathor knew, though he might not have been able to say so in so many words. Lord Threnod was one of those who rule by bluff and bluster, by cruelty and conniving, until those beneath him submit or rebel. Despite the yoke that bound him and the chain by which he was dragged, Hathor vowed to himself to be one who fought rather than yielded. Just for good measure he stopped short and dug in his heels as they reached the dirt-covered courtyard, causing the guard who hauled him to come up short and fall backward.

"Come on, you oversize eyesore." Just before it came cracking down on his back, Hathor saw the short whip in Lord Threnod's hand, but too late to grab at the lashing cord, which was not a thin stinging strip of leather but a thick one, knotted on the end, designed to leave painful unseen welts rather than flay the skin.

"My men wish to see prodigious feats of strength. Will you oblige them?" Lord Threnod shouted in Hathor's ear as the besieged troll knelt under repeated blows from the ball-ended whip.

If that was all they wanted, Hathor would do it, but he suspected elsewise. The off-duty guards, somewhat depleted from yesterday's battle, encircled him in the center of the court. They were a vengeful lot, and some tried to kick out at him or beat him, but a few growls and some chain-rattling discouraged them. A medium-size boulder was brought out. He lifted it easily. A timber beam was produced. Hathor hefted it without strain.

"No wonder we suffered such losses. Do you use a piercing axe or a felling axe?" one of the captains of the guard asked him, a burly man with fine red hair like Hathor's.

"I use a wood axe," Hathor answered simply, as was his nature. This drew a laugh from Lord Threnod.

"Indeed, you splintered a good bit of kindling yesterday."

A tug-of-war was organized, Hathor against five of the guard. He toppled them like draughts pegs.

"Bring out the Bog Man," the guardsmen clamored, while Hathor, baffled by the reference, stood in the center of the aroused crowd, his restraining chain now fastened to an iron ring atop an iron post spiked into the hard-packed earth of the interior plaza. With none to whom he could turn for help, Hathor simply put his head down like a draft animal and waited patiently for the next challenge.

"The Bog Man, the Bog Man!" the mob of soldiers begged their lord, but apparently Lord Threnod was unwilling to risk injury to his prize possession.

"They would kill each other," was all the false lord would say in demurring to honor the request. To gain his freedom, Hathor would have fought anyone or anything.

"Who is this Bog?" he wondered, but Lord Threnod had come up with another test of Hathor's strength to amuse his men.

"Carry me," he ordered. Chained to the planted stake, Hathor could go nowhere, but he obliged by lifting Lord Threnod up onto his shoulders. Apparently Lord Threnod did not fear that Hathor would throw him—he kicked at Hathor's ribs like a child playing at horse.

"Hur, hur, up horse." Hathor cantered around the iron pole at the end of his shackles. The metal bonds creaked and scraped against each other. The humiliated troll had now been made to act the part of a dog on a leash and a riding horse, much to the delight of Threnod's troops, who howled and taunted Hathor mercilessly.

"Get up there, pony!"

"Trot, beast, or we'll make a horse stew out of you."

They are brave today, when I am alone and in irons, Hathor thought, remembering the day before when his four had taken on a hundred and more and nearly won.

Finally Lord Threnod tired of these bloodless amusements. Relenting to the repeated entreaties of his men, he ordered the Bog Man to be brought out: "—for one fall only, and we'll have to muzzle and declaw them first." At that Hathor felt himself grabbed from behind by four men who pushed him roughly to the ground. While they held him, a fifth man fastened Hathor's mighty grinding jaws shut with strips of leather like a horse's bit and bridle. Then he pulled small burlap sacks stuffed with chicken feathers over Hathor's thick-fingered hands, and tied them on at the wrists. Thus encumbered, Hathor could neither bite nor punch effectively.

He was hauled to his feet again just as another group of guards emerged from the door to the cellar dungeons with a foul-smelling shape, also in chains, a large-looming lump of life, vaguely human-looking, with two arms, two legs, a torso, and a head, but all swollen and puffed, as if a corpse had lain in a bog soaking up the bog juices for many a long year, and then risen again. Its eyes were lifeless, yet it walked and breathed, after a fashion, gulping the air in heaving gasps as though it labored for each lungful. It wore a prisoner's sackcloth shirt that trailed down to its protuberant knees. When it reached the ring where Hathor stood, it too was fitted with restraints on its hands and gagged. Hathor felt a kindred sadness for it.

"Ye gods, I don't know which one stinks the worse. You could take wagers and make a contest of that!" Lord Threnod shouted. His men cheered. There was some argument as to how to have them fight—no one wanted to risk unchaining either of them. Finally it was decided to lie them down and let them leg wrestle. The advantage there seemed to go to Hathor, with his immense lower body, bulging thighs and calves, but the Bog Man, distended and cadaverous as he was, possessed some demonic strength. Hathor sensed the power of one who does not fear death, because he is already beyond it. *He cannot hurt himself*, was the way Hathor thought of it.

Hathor knew the rules. They were to lay down alongside each other on their backs, head to foot, so that they could lift and lock legs and wrestle. He wasn't sure the Bog Man knew what was expected of him, but Lord Threnod assured him that the Bog Man was an experienced combatant.

"In fact he has never lost since we acquired him," Lord Threnod informed Hathor.

The two unlikely wrestlers took their positions, awkwardly arranging their chains to free themselves as much as possible. Lord Threnod, with his gruesome sense of humor, proposed a reward for the winner.

"Let the winner eat the loser!" someone shouted to the delight of the excited throng, but Threnod was still mindful of his investment; all he offered was double rations of the soupy gruel Hathor had received the night before. That watery cereal had been his only meal since the interrupted feast in the Hall of Shields, of which he had partaken only of the cakes and ale, in any case. Hungry, tired, and sore, Hathor looked up at the sky wearily and wished it was a fortnight ago, and that he was back in his snug cave, warm and sluggish. Fortunately, it was his right leg he wrestled with, while it was the left that had received the stab wound just before he was netted the day before. The knife had passed between muscle and bone, narrowly missing both and sinking itself into the fleshy part of Hathor's thigh, so it hardly impeded him. When his leg first touched the Bog Man's, Hathor recoiled. Its flesh was cold and moldering. How did such a being remain alive, if it was truly alive? But when they intertwined and braced at the knee for the contest, Hathor felt a surge of inhuman power course through the Bog Man. As Hathor had suspected, the creature could exert himself beyond the limits of mortal endurance. It felt no pain.

Leg-wrestling matches are usually over in seconds, as it is difficult to maintain balance once one side or the other gains an advantage. The two fighters in this match, however, had such broad backs and were so nearly equal in strength that neither gained an immediate edge. Each with a leg upraised they grunted and huffed while the soldiers of Lord Threnod raised mock cheers for one or the other, and flung coins at each other in their haste to place bets on the outcome.

After the struggle had continued for some time, Hathor realized that the Bog Man was toying with him—Hathor could never defeat his ghoulish opponent, who employed only enough resistance to keep his leg even with Hathor's. The incentive of cold mush was not what drove the Bog Man—Hathor doubted that the living corpse even ate food. What kept it upright and active, he could not even guess. Why then was he playing this foolish and dangerous game with the impatient Lord Threnod and his revenge-seeking troops?

The constant strain began to take its toll on Hathor's depleted strength. Though he hated to lose, he could see no hope of victory, and no reason to maintain the meaningless stalemate the Bog Man seemed to favor. It seemed pointless to remain locked in futile resistance to his silent adversary, who had neither looked at him nor made a sound other than his labored breathing. But something in Hathor's stubborn troll nature refused to let him give in. He continued to push against his implacable foe, who merely equaled Hathor's increased pressure with its own.

As the deadlock persisted, the audience grew bored and disgusted by the inactivity and lack of result. They booed and spit at the two weary competitors, but the impasse continued. By twos and threes the crowd dwindled away, as soldiers were called to duty or simply lost interest, until there were only a half dozen or so left to watch and stand guard. Then, as Hathor strained to keep his equilibrium, the Bog Man spoke to Hathor for the first time. Somehow he had chewed his way through the cloth gag, or had the acidic bog juices that flowed through his veins instead of blood eaten through it?

"When they come in to release us, kill me," he whispered to Hathor. Startled, Hathor raised his head and looked the Bog Man full in the face. The pleading expression in those vacant eyes clutched at Hathor's heart. "Free me, kill me," the thing begged again in a murmur. Imagining himself consigned to a similar fate, Hathor wondered if he too would beseech a stranger for the reprieve of death, true death, not the walking, living hell in which the Bog Man wandered alone. Suddenly he realized that the long standoff was the Bog Man's simple plan to give Hathor a few seconds, without the crowd surrounding them, time enough to kill him. What horror, to prefer death to life. But was what the Bog Man endured really life?

In an instant the Bog Man relaxed its pressure and Hathor's leg swung down over his yielding opponent. Quickly Hathor looped the chain around the unresisting Bog Man's

neck and drew it tight, crushing the creature's windpipe.
Soldiers rushed in, beating Hathor about the head, but he
kept his clumsily bound hands on the chain until he saw the
lackluster eyes dim and freeze. The enlarged face, already
a sickly green, turned purple as the remaining air in his
overworked lung was used up. Lord Threnod, who kept the
Bog Man for bizarre and unknown purposes, or perhaps just
from curiosity over the aberrant brute, was enraged that his
pet had been destroyed.

"You won! Why did you have to slay him too? Oh, I
suppose I understand," Lord Threnod grudgingly relented,
as he too was a warrior, and not knowing Hathor's true
motive, he had mistaken Hathor's sudden murderous act as
the savage exultation of the victor over the vanquished. "But
you must pay, for I paid dearly to get him. Now what would
be suitable punishment? No, I cannot decide immediately. I
must think on this. Take them away." Hathor was led back
up to his eyrie cell, the Bog Man to a final resting place he
richly deserved.

Hathor received no gruel for dinner that night, no food
or water at all, but in the morning Lord Threnod paid him
another personal visit, though Hathor had woken himself
early to avoid a stunning soaking at his captor's hands. This
time he managed to catch and lap up some of the hurled
liquid.

"Very clever, for a block-headed inhuman creature. You
killed one of my pets. That was very bad. But I have
concluded that no penalty I could devise would be greater
than the one your new owner has prepared for you," Lord
Threnod said gleefully, again alluding to Hathor's fate, "so
I will do nothing, for now. However, I shall put in an order,
at the appropriate time, and you shall know it comes from
me," he told the uncomprehending troll.

Today was the day he was to meet his new master. After
his early morning visit from Lord Threnod, Hathor was left
alone until an hour before the purchaser's anticipated arrival. At that time he was dragged from his cell to a cistern

within the castle, where he was forcibly bathed to remove the caked blood, mud, and grime of the last two days. Aside from a few black and blue marks and the still-healing thigh wound, Hathor was in decent physical shape. A few good meals and some rest would see him well again, if he got them. After his bath they doused him with some sweet perfume to mask his natural scent, but even so the dogs let loose with a storm of howls when he and his guard passed the kennels on the way to be presented to Lord Threnod.

"Charming!" was the imperious lord's comment. "See that he is provided a decent set of clothes." Other than that, Lord Threnod hardly acknowledged Hathor's presence. Apparently he had moved on to weightier matters, like how he was going to maintain his duchy without support and revenue from the townspeople. Already the stocks of salted fish and crabs were dissipated, and worse, the ale casks were running low. With the coin he expected to secure for Hathor, Lord Threnod could get by for a while, but not forever.

Hathor was led away to a holding cell on the ground floor. He rubbed a handful of dirt on himself to try to rid the sickly sweet scent of perfume from his nostrils, but it was useless.

Worse than a skunk, he thought. Suddenly there was a flourish of sackbuts and cornets (Lord Threnod did love his music) announcing the arrival of a visitor. Hathor was rushed from the temporary confinement to the center of the plaza, between rows of soldiers dressed in their finest battle gear. Some of the prized shields from the Hall of Shields had been unhung and brought out to add to the pomp of the occasion. The iron bars of the main gate were drawn back noisily and the portal creaked open on its massive hinges. When the stranger entered, Lord Threnod's troops fell away unconsciously, and the dogs on display drew back with bared fangs and low growls, their ears pinned to their heads but their tails between their legs in a mixture of fear and ferociousness. The object of their strange behavior was the leader of a cortege draped in black. Black-hooded soldiers accompanied a stout black carriage, so large it was like a prison cell on wheels. Wooden slats formed walls. There was a heavy door on one wall of the contraption, but no windows. At the head of the procession was the leader, a smallish man also dressed in black—black boots, a black cape, and a mask and cowl of black—so that he looked less human than an apparition, a dark portent of some unseen evil.

Evidently Lord Threnod was not on such good terms with this personage as he had boasted to Hathor. The suddenly timid lord approached his guest uncertainly, not sure whether to bluster or bow: "I had expected my friend Lazvic the Trader. I had no idea that an emissary of the Master himself would—" Lord Threnod began, only to be interrupted by a command from the man in black:

"Hand over your prisoner."

"Just like that, then?" Taken aback, Lord Threnod could only sputter an order to his sergeant-at-arms, and before he could turn again and face his cryptic guest, the becaped stranger had withdrawn into the carriage to await the presentation of Hathor.

"Well!" Lord Threnod mumbled, and gestured to his men to place Hathor in the boxy wheeled cage. He tried to peek in as Hathor was shoved into the vehicle, but his view was blocked by the black-shrouded horsemen who crowded round the transfer, their dusky horses stamping and snorting at the scent of the troll. Stepping back to avoid being trampled, Lord Threnod swore and cursed and demanded his payment. A bag of coins was tossed at his feet. Lord Threnod stooped unceremoniously to pick it up and was kicked in the backside by a nervous steed.

"Ooof!" he wheezed as he fell and landed on the money sack, knocking the wind out of himself. From inside, Hathor, peering through a crack in the slats, laughed when he saw Lord Threnod rubbing his rear.

Lord Threnod pounded on the side of the wagon. "Laugh now, you benighted monster. Where you go there is no laughter."

Then a tarpaulin was cast over the box, further shutting Hathor off from the world. It was almost cavelike inside, Hathor thought, except for the jolting motion of the rig over the rough road leading down and away from Steadfast-by-Sea. Hathor lay back and tried to imagine his friends, still alive, somewhere at sea, but the rocking soon lulled his weary troll's brain to sleep.

CHAPTER
8

All day the carriage rolled north. Hathor, whose sense of direction was not strong, knew that it must be north by one sign only: the road traveled along the edge of the water, and the lapping water noise was on his right. Anyway, Lord Threnod had made no secret of the fact that his guest was a Northerner, and indeed everything right from the start, including the direction Endril had led them in and the information they had heard about the goings-on near Dripping Hall, all pointed in that direction.

His captors were not the Wind-Websters, of that Hathor was certain. For all the mystery surrounding those lords and their cloud-shrouded lands, they were not like the grim warriors who possessed Hathor now. No, these were emissaries from some other demesne, some other realm, perhaps from the source of the Mistwall itself, for all Hathor knew. Because he knew he was destined for some living fate, he did not fear for his life, and the darkness of the inside of the wagon-box soothed him, but still his mind was troubled by thoughts of his lost comrades, and of the poor villagers who had unsuccessfully tried to overthrow

Lord Threnod. The village (by harvesting the fruits of the sea beyond) had been the source of Lord Threnod's wealth, yet he allowed his soldiers to destroy it. Why? Why were lords so often willing to sacrifice the lives and property of others to save their own?

"Grrrr!" Hathor grumbled to himself. "Too much for me to think about."

At evening the wagon stopped and after a while the tarp was thrown back, a slit opened up on the door and a bone was thrown in to him. Hathor shrugged his shoulders uselessly. How could he explain to them, when he barely understood himself his own motives for giving up meat, except that he was trying to become a better troll, to improve himself, to rise from sub-hume darkness to some deeper sense of the world and his place in it.

He examined the bone without touching it. Bits of flesh still clung to it, but it had an odd texture, as if it had been aged—suddenly Hathor realized that it was from the leg of the Bog Man, bog-cured and preserved even before its corporeal death. Hathor shuddered to think what had become of the rest of the Bog Man. Perhaps even now the black-dressed soldiers outside were enjoying a soup or stew of its body parts. It could easily have been him in the pot, Hathor realized, and he remembered an old troll saying: "What he would have done to me, I did to him."

His appetite diminished by the nauseating sight, Hathor slumped to the floor with his back against one wall of the wagon and tried to sleep, but he had been sleeping all day and now his thoughts were scattered and troublesome. He called for his guards to remove the grotesque meal, but they ignored him. After a time he squinted through the slats to see what was going on in the camp. To his surprise, the soldiers were not bedding down, but instead were clearing the remains of the ghastly repast and preparing to ride again. Apparently they were going to push on through the night. With the heavy wagon plodding through rough roads made muddy by the recent rains, the going had been slow

even in daylight. Several times the troops had been forced
to dismount to lever the wheels out of deep sucking ruts.
Why they would risk a night march was beyond Hathor.

"Hey," he called to the nearest horsemen, "why do we
go at night?"

"Because of you, you cursed cur," was the insulting
reply.

"I am in no hurry," Hathor made a small joke, but the
soldier ignored him, intent on adjusting his riding equipment.

"Let me out and I will pull the wagon and save your
horses," Hathor offered, but the same rider told him he had
spooked the horses enough already with his stink. No one
loved him. No one wanted him. His only friends in life
were either dead or far off at sea, beyond helping him, and
they would never find him where he was going, wherever
that was. As Hathor brooded, the world seemed to close in
on him, weighing down on him, becoming dim, then black,
but it was only the covering being refitted over the outside
of the wagon-top.

They traveled for a week. Each day was the same for
Hathor. Each morn he was let out to relieve himself; each
evening he was provided a scrap of bone or hunk of rotting
meat that he did not eat. During his morning respite, Hathor
foraged listlessly in the bushes for something edible—once
he found a handful of berries, but they were the astringent
kind that made his cheeks pucker and his lips turn purple and
he spat them out. The morning hunger was the worst. Each
time he returned to the wagon the uneaten rations had been
removed, so that even if he had broken his vow, he could not
have done so 'til nightfall, by which time he had convinced
himself again that he could go without for another night.
The memory of the Bog Man and the sight of the tainted
victuals were enough to strengthen his resolve, but when
he woke in the morning he hungered again. He subsisted
then on the faintly salty water he was allotted, supplanted
by an occasional twig, berry, or root he scrounged from the

scrubby seaside vegetation during the daybreak rest stops. His tireless captors rode almost ceaselessly. Not once in seven days did they camp for the night. Instead, they would break for two hours at dawn and dusk, then remount and ride all night. Hathor marveled at their stamina, and that of the horses. Wherever these people were from, they were a hardy, healthy bunch. Their sinister appearance and their cold, unfeeling treatment of Hathor did not deter Hathor from feeling at least a little better for having escaped the clutches of Lord Threnod, who seemed to enjoy the cruelty he inflicted. These were merely soldiers obeying orders and doing a job—Hathor could understand that.

On the third or fourth day—Hathor had lost track in the blanketed darkness of his captivity—he befriended the youngest rider, a new recruit who was assigned to ride with the wagon because he could not keep up with the vanguard while learning how to control the rambunctious roan gelding he had been assigned to ride.

As he rode beside the wagon, the youngster sang to himself, which made Hathor think immediately of Bith. Though he could not see the youth, Hathor imagined him as fuzzy-cheeked and fair—his voice cracked like one just coming to manhood. Hathor, usually recalcitrant and not given to making the first gesture of communication, had been cooped up in the wagon for long enough that he craved a little conversation. He tried the youth.

"Guardsman. Do ye know the ballad of Osric and Eanfled?" Hathor asked, mentioning the song Bith had sung and played on the crwth for Lord Threnod.

"Shut up, you beast," the young man answered, and Hathor knew that he had been commanded not to converse with the prisoner, for there was no spiteful conviction in his voice, instead an almost apologetic tone.

"I'm no beast, though I'm not a bloody hume, thanks be to the gods! What harm have I ever done you?" Hathor wanted to know, and almost at once the boy offered his repentance.

"None, poor soul. Forgive me, I am under orders." He fell silent.

"Can't you throw off this sheet, so I get air?" Hathor asked, for truly the black drape trapped the sunlight and made it insufferably warm within.

"I cannot."

"Why is everything black—why do you wear black?"

"For warmth. Where we live 'tis so cold we need all the heat we can muster. So we wear black unless we hunt on the ice, where we must blend in and hide from our quarry."

"What do you hunt?"

"The Shaggy White Bear—ten feet tall and very fierce."

"I've heard of it," Hathor said, though he had not.

"No more questions now. I am forbidden to talk with you, low one."

The boy reminded Hathor of Cal in more ways than one. His impetuosity, his vacillation between friendliness and hostility, his youthful demeanor, all brought his lost companion to mind.

"Am I to be hunted?" Hathor asked simply. The youth did not know, or would not say.

"No more questions," he repeated, and at that moment another rider fell back from the main group ahead and sidled up beside the young guard.

Each day the wind came through the planks a little fresher and chillier. Each day seemed to grow longer and each night thus shorter, so that by the end of a week there seemed to be no evening at all, only an endless twilight in which they rode endlessly. On the sixth day the party left the shore of the Sea of Storms and turned inland, but still heading roughly north, across a flat featureless plain unknown to Hathor. The wind was now a clever sprite that worked its way between the slats of his cage and nipped at his red hair and beard. Because he had been stripped of his heavy coat by Lord Threnod, and dressed hurriedly for his presentation to his new owner, Hathor was ill-fit for cold weather. He complained to the young guard whom he was still trying to befriend, by degrees. Thus far Hathor had not been able to gain his trust.

"Thrydwulf," (for that was his name—this much Hathor had learned) "I am cold."

"I cannot help you. I have only my own coat and a bedroll."

"Some berries or grass, then, to warm my belly."

"What? You get a larger ration of meat than the troops each meal."

"I don't eat it." Hathor explained to Thrydwulf that he would not eat the meat he was given, that he craved vegetables and fruits.

"Oh, my grandmama had the same trouble when she lost her teeth," Thrydwulf sympathized. Through the hole in the cage door Hathor showed Thrydwulf that his oversize yellow troll's teeth were in fine working order. He disclosed that it was a deliberate decision on his part to forgo meat, and that he was hungry.

"Well, a trade, then. I'll take your portion of meat and bring you whatever I can forage."

"Agreed."

"I warn you though, not much grows on the ice plain, a few blue groundberries and some scrubby chokecherry bushes."

"I'll take what you bring," Hathor replied, for he was sorely hungry after almost a week without food.

That night Thrydwulf secretly passed Hathor a handful of roots and berries, scarcely a meal and mixed with moss and twigs and humus earth, but Hathor devoured it clods of dirt and all.

"Thank you, young friend."

"It's a poor life you go to, troll. I pity you."

"Do not pity me. I will live."

"Don't be so sure. My ruler is ruthless."

"He looks hume enough to me," said Hathor, who had had some experience with these things.

It was Thrydwulf's turn to say, "What do you mean? You haven't seen our regent yet."

"He rides at the head of your group—a tall man in a cape."

"That is only our captain. No, your owner is ahead, in the castle, waiting for you. When you arrive, you will understand." There was something Thrydwulf was not telling him, Hathor realized, but he couldn't guess what it was.

"But Lord Threnod said—" Hathor, confused, fell silent. So, he had been misled by Lord Threnod. A hume had lied to him again. *Why can't they say the simple truth, as trolls do: "Get out of my way," or "I will eat you." Wouldn't that be more honest than the way of these humes? Instead they hem and haw and smile at you and then tell lies to your face.*

"What does it matter?" Thrydwulf was saying to him, and Hathor had to agree. Now or later, he would meet his master.

It was now so cold that Hathor had to stamp around in his cage as they traveled, or the wind would climb inside his thin clothes and torture him with fingers of ice. Outside it snowed almost every day, and even when it wasn't snowing the sky was a threatening grey. Hathor rubbed himself vigorously, beating his arms and clapping himself on his shoulders with crossed hands. It was the lot of all prisoners in these times to be roughly treated. Once, in earlier days, or was it only among trolls, there had been a kinder way of doing things, to Hathor's mind. Either you were killed and possibly eaten immediately, or you were freed. There were no prisoners. That was before the hume notion of ransom took sway.

These humes and their money-grubbing ways, Hathor griped as he paced, sometimes stumbling as the cart skidded on a patch of ice or heaved upward on a frost bump. *If they can't make a coin on it, it is worthless to them.* In the old days, Hathor made do on barter, along with a little theft and pillage. The farmers' rotten turnips he took now were

nothing to the lambkins and squealing little porkers he lifted
before. But what was he thinking! Was he slipping back to
his former ways in the absence of duty? Without Bith to
protect and a mission to strive for, Hathor felt lost. But
wait! Hadn't he taken an oath? He still had a mission to
fulfill, even if his companions were not there to aid him.
Now what was it? Hathor searched his cloudy memory for
the reason they had ventured north. It had something to do
with a rip in the Mistwall, and—oh, yes, he himself was
important to the mission. He'd been singled out, and hadn't
it worked out that way?

With new resolve Hathor put a little snap into his walk,
trying to remember how Cal had taught him that soldiers
march, with clicking precision; but his heavy feet would
not keep time to his ragged counting. After a while he resumed his prisoner's shuffle, but in his heart there burned a
new fervor. He would conquer this wizard, then he would
turn south and search the world over, even cross the Sea
of Storms into lands unknown, to find Bith and the others.
Until then, he had to trust that Cal and Endril could do the
job he, Hathor, had appointed for himself, of guarding the
princess Bith. If they were still alive.

The drear plain gradually gave way to a forested region,
still cold and flat but infinitely less numbing to the body
and mind than the open sweep they had been crossing for
almost a week. Snow hung on the giant firs that lined their
route, occasionally cascading off a bent bough in miniature
avalanches. On the first night into the woods they were met
by a greeting party from wherever it was they were going,
(Hathor had yet to learn the name of the place). The wagon
was fitted with runners of wood curled at the tips, and the
horses were sent south and a pack of dogs brought by the
vanguard were hitched to the wagon in their place. Once
again there was a tense moment as the wolfish-looking dogs
caught wind of Hathor inside, and bared their fangs and laid
their ears low and growled, but a few icy lashings of a whip
above their heads turned them around in their traces, and

within an hour of the meeting they were on their way again, the wagon gliding easily across the snow depths of the forest while the dismounted men struggled behind in the drifts. The soldiers had fitted themselves with oversize shoes of wooden frames webbed with leather strips that strapped onto their boots, but even with these devices they floundered in the deep snow.

On the plain the blowing snow did not accumulate, but here in the forest there were little dells and knolls everywhere. Though none were higher than a few feet, they trapped the snow in deep piles, so that one minute the soldiers might be walking on bare ground, and the next be hip deep in heaped snow. They seemed to enjoy it, though. Hathor could hear them next to the wagon (they could no longer ride proudly ahead) playfully tossing handfuls of the stuff at each other like boys, and sliding down the smallest hills on their backsides, until the stern captain called them to order again and they resumed a uniform march file.

The pleasant forest turned out to be only a brief respite between the harshness of the ice plain and the land they entered next. From within his moving cell Hathor could not see the mountains coming, but he felt the pitch of the wagon shift as they began climbing abruptly and steeply into a wilderness of giant boulders and needlelike pinnacles of frozen rock. Within a mile the elevation rose several hundred feet. Immense icicles hung everywhere from jutting cliffs overhanging the roadway, which hugged the mountainside and followed a twisting path upward, coiling back on itself at every opportunity. Hathor, his face pressed to the narrow crack in the cage door, caught a frightening glimpse of the sheer drop-away below him as the wagon slid precariously close to the cliff edge on one turn.

As the incline grew steeper the dogs struggled and finally the men had to take up the toil. They lashed ropes to the front of the wagon and slung them over their shoulders, six men on a line, but even then they barely inched forward.

The combined weight of the wagon and Hathor was too much for them.

"Let me out and I'll pull it up myself," Hathor offered, but having come this far the troops dared not risk losing their cargo. Late in the afternoon of the seventh day of the trip, by a great effort of painful pushes and pulls, and a healthy application of melted wax on the wagon runners (instead of lifting the wagon they melted the wax in front of it and drove the vehicle over the hot puddle), the soldiers in black eventually crested the ridge before them onto a surprisingly flat bluff beneath the final crag where the palace stood. This lower ledge was the soldiers' permanent encampment, a bustling village of tents and wooden shacks that nestled up against the power wall of the palace. The dogs were taken from their harnesses, leashed, and fed and the soldiers' campfires started before the wagon was finally dragged off to a corner of the camp where a few other wagons were stored. In the early evening, just as Hathor began to think that they had forgotten about him, a detachment of twenty came for him. He was once again put in chains. Hathor offered no resistance. He was weak from hunger, bruised from the bumpy trip in the crude cart, and tired. Rubbing his eyes even in the fading light, he stumbled out of the cell and allowed himself to be shackled in manacles without so much as a menacing growl. He looked around the camp. Except for its position on its wide ledge above the forest and beneath the higher promontory, it was like many others Hathor had seen before, the raggedy, never-really-settled squatters' town of soldiers always on the move. The camp followers, the cooks and laundrywomen, the wives and prostitutes and children and dogs of the military men lived in perpetual upheaval. They might move once a month, or never, but still the camp would remain a camp, never quite a village or town, rootless, dusty, and like the swirling dust always ready to be swept away by the wind.

Hathor gazed up at the palace above. Yes, it was always like this. The soldiers lived apart from those they served, as if they were not good enough, yet who won the victories that provided those inside the palace their luxurious lives? Who fought and died that they might sip wine in warmth and comfort and safety? Yet soldiers never complained. They went where they were told, did what they were told to do, and huddled in front of their campfires on nights like tonight, dreaming of life in the palace above but never thinking that they might actually achieve it.

Oof! What fools we all are, Hathor thought to himself as he was led under irons (again) toward the base of sheer wall, for he considered himself much like these paid mercenaries, as one who always worked in the service of others and had little for himself. Yet with his three companions he had tasted as much of a sense of freedom as he had ever known, wandering the countryside as a doer of good. Never much of one to accumulate possessions, he appreciated the simple life the camp-dwellers led, who could pick up and put everything on their backs and move on an instant's notice. The smell of roasting meat drifted toward him as he approached the lower gate, and although it did not tempt him, the aroma made him look even more fondly at the ragtag settlement. Somewhere his almost-friend Thrydwulf must be reunited with family or friends, all glad that he has come home safely from another march, another battle, another war. They would give him the best joints of meat, place him at the head of the fire, listen to his stories of lands far off and creatures strange. *Yes, look, they have brought back one of the monsters, me, Hathor,* the homesick and friendless troll thought in a fit of melancholy.

This gate, a portal carved into the stone wall of the mountain, was equipped with a portcullis that had to be raised by cranking a winch. Behind the portcullis was an iron door, and behind that door a second, with a space between them where invaders could be trapped and with holes in the ceiling for pouring melted lead on their heads. As soon as they entered through the second door, all remaining daylight was lost, and the way ahead narrowed and shrank into a tunnel.

A set of stairs cut directly into the stone led upward in an uneven spiral. The passageway was tight for the soldiers and nearly impassable for Hathor. It was lighted by torches shoved into crevices in the rock. Smoke hung in the stifled air, making visibility even poorer. Hathor began to cough from the torch fumes, and he tripped on the hacked stone stairs, but the soldiers, who disliked the confining staircase, shoved him forward. Around and around they went, up and around, up and around. Once they came upon a slit window. Hathor grabbed a quick breath of fresh air and a glimpse of the campsite below, but the soldiers did not care to be stuck in the passageway behind the smelly troll, so they prodded him along before he could really recover from the smoke and the dank air. They struggled another hundred steps up, with the fleeting memory of the vista beyond the camp lingering in Hathor's brain—the green forest spreading away, and beyond, like a vast ocean, the flowing horizon of the white plain they had crossed, that led to the northern edge of the Sea of Storms.

At the top of the rock-hewn interior staircase was a sentry post, another portcullis, and a second iron door. Beyond, Hathor could see the empty cavern of the strangely deserted palace, its high-vaulted ceiling lost in dim reaches high above, its icy walls gleaming in the half-light. It was like no place Hathor had ever been, a fantastic cave many times the size of his tiny burrow. Instead of the trappings of wealth and royalty Hathor had expected, there was a barren grimness to the foreboding and stark void that composed the center of the space, like an abandoned killing ground.

Who or what were the earnest sentries guarding? Hathor was handed over to the upper sentinels. The soldiers who had brought him to this desolate place turned on their heels and scampered down the stairs as if they couldn't flee the morbid atmosphere quickly enough. Hathor envied them. In a few minutes they would join Thrydwulf and the others at the warmth and camaraderie of fireside in the camp. But then there was no more time for reflection as Hathor was led, still chained, to the center of the magnificent grotto. The perimeter of the gigantic cavity was ringed with flaming torches like the tunnel passageway, but the smoke drifted up and out of holes cut in the ceiling, through which Hathor could see the first shy stars of evening glowing uncertainly. The whole eastern wall overlooking the camp opened onto space. Opposite this entrance, at the back of the cave, a massive throne chair carved out of the same rock was the only man-made object in the room, and even it was practically part and parcel of the unbroken flow of floor and wall.

Hathor's chain was fastened to a ringed spike like the one he'd been clasped to when he fought the Bog Man, but here there were no crowds. The guards slipped back into the darkness at the outer edge of the room, and Hathor was left standing alone, his huge frame dwarfed by the immensity of the cave.

"Halloo?" he called, but his voice bounced unanswered down unseen tunnels in many directions. Turning, he faced the grand opening at the mouth of the cave. From there the panorama he had sighted from the slit window would be in full view. From this height Hathor imagined that one might even be able to see all the way across the plain to the Sea of Storms itself, but the short lead prevented him from approaching the opening. Weary and beaten, Hathor sat down facing the cave mouth and coiled the iron links of his chain in his lap. As he sat, he heard a fine rustling behind him, but there were always scuttling and fluttering noises in a cave, and Hathor paid it no attention until he felt a sharp poke in his back. When he turned around he was facing the Queen of Ice.

"Welcome to our little corner of the world," she began, while Hathor stared in awe at her splendid black dress, bejeweled with ice crystals that sparkled and blazed in the torchlight, at her raven hair and luminous black eyes, at the furry black creature she held in her arms, petting and stroking it as she talked. Regally thin, she was nearly as tall as Hathor at a third his weight, but a malign strength emanated from her presence, a frosty power that made Hathor shudder involuntarily.

"Are you cold, my warm-blooded one? You had better get used to it."

"Lord Threnod said master, not mistress—" As usual, Hathor spoke simply and directly, without using formal address or making a bow, but the queen took no notice.

"Lord Threnod, that fat useless bumblekin, is an idiot! Tell us, are there many like you?"

"In some places there are many of my kind," Hathor answered.

"No, no, we mean, are there many who are giving up the eating of flesh?"

"No others, that I know of."

"Good. We mean to keep it that way. Tell us, why do you do this?"

Hathor shook his head wearily. The repeated question wore on him. Why couldn't people leave him alone to follow the dictates of his own heart?

"Something inside me told me it was right." Then Hathor asked her the question he asked of anyone he thought might have an answer: "How can it be right to kill innocent and helpless animals?"

"A priggish, morally superior troll. What a scandal!" the queen hissed with displeasure. "Tell us, O virtuous one, have you seen a vegetable, even a miserable root vegetable growing in the last fifty miles? If you lived up here you'd be a meat-eater too! Yes! Meat! Strength! The wolf eats the lamb!" The queen raged and thrust her angry face in Hathor's docile one. Hathor saw that she was old, very old, though her black hair and slenderness and the tight-fitting black gown made her look younger from a distance. "Yes, you'd be chewing blubber like the rest of us, for life and warmth. And you will. Mark our words. You will. We intend to make you repent of your vows."

"Where will you keep me?" Hathor asked.

"You will not stay here. No, we have hired you out to our friends the Wind-Websters. We are in league, you might say. What we tell them to do, they do, and the same for you."

At last Hathor had something to cheer about. The Wind-Websters! So, they were involved after all. The trail grew warm, the scent freshened. Though he was alone and enchained, he was approaching the goal the four had set out for themselves.

"—and we do not keep you, you earn your keep, yes, in a very special way. We are sure you will do a good job of it. We'll even give you back an axe, for we have heard you are fond of them and quite handy with one."

You make a mistake if you do that, Hathor thought to himself, but said nothing to the queen. *Even in chains I stand a chance with an axe in my hands!* The imperious woman must have read his simple thoughts: she laughed and put down the squirming animal, which ran off into the darkness before Hathor could tell what it was.

"There will be no escape for you. We are not the fool Threnod is, and we have no intention of losing any men to your axe-wielding hands. No, you will willingly give up the tool at the end of your workday, I warrant." Hathor doubted he would voluntarily relinquish his beloved weapon once he regained it, but then his attention was captured by the sight of the queen ascending to her stone throne. It was much too large for her, so that when she sat down she looked like a child in an adult's chair—her feet did not reach to the stone floor.

She spoke again, without favoring Hathor with so much as a glance: "This seat of power was bequeathed to us by the giants who used to occupy this mountain. Before we killed them we made them tell us the secrets of their abode. This throne is more than a chair, it is a wellspring, a source of rejuvenation, not for low-born such as you of course, but for magicians and royalty such as ourselves."

The suggestion rankled the heart of the guileless troll. "Why do you call yourself 'we'?" he asked. "To me you are only another horrible hume."

"Because we are great, and it is our prerogative, you mannerless beast. You know nothing of the customs of court, you are lower than the meanest serf or peasant, yet you stand before us and do not bow your head in respect, and then you challenge the royal 'we.' Insubordinate. No matter. We will suborn you. In two weeks you will be as tame as a lamb led to slaughter."

It was a strange scene, the rough-looking troll standing alone and manacled, immersed in moonlight streaming in from the cave opening, the queen talking down to him from her oversize throne, the guards lurking in the shadows, fearful of Hathor even bound as he was. Before the queen called an end to the proceedings, she let slip to Hathor the essence of her plan, though it would be weeks before he understood the significance of the words she pronounced then:

"When the cold comes in, men turn thin, their hearts mirror the weather. Mark our words. What comes through the Mistwall does not return."

With a slight motion of her hand she called for the guards, who came forward and led Hathor away. He turned to look back and saw the Queen of Ice still seated on the throne. Her pet had climbed up to join her, and she stroked it steadily, singing to herself like a madwoman. The weird image haunted his dreams that night, as he slept on a pallet of straw in yet another prison cell.

CHAPTER
9

Cal kicked at the gunwales of the boat and cursed the limp sail above his head. For three days they had floated nowhere, becalmed on a glass-smooth sea. In the rush to flee Lord Threnod's men, no one had bothered to load provisions—the tiny fleet was sorely in need of water and food, though the crafty fishermen had captured some rainwater in leather funnels during the wild storm that had sent them flying away from their home, and they could catch as much fish as they wanted from their sturdy and well-rigged fishing boats. Other staples such as vegetables, flour, salt, and sugar were in short supply.

"Why don't you blow us up another storm, Bith," Cal suggested. Not for him was this damnable waiting, this aimless drifting under a marine sun that cracked his skin and parched his lips and burned under his eyelids.

"I could," Bith answered in a muffled voice from her resting spot under a canvas sack in the forepeak. "But I have no idea where it might drive us, or for how long or how fast."

"Mmmmm—" Endril joined in, "I think one wind spell

is enough. We were lucky not to have swamped the boats in that last one. Once during the tempest I looked up over the rail and saw a forty-footer rising above my head. I thought sure it was going to break on deck and wash us all away, but these villagers are as much magicians at the helm as Bith is at her craft."

"Indeed!" Cal exclaimed. "That was a fine bit of sailing in a squall, but now what is needed is more action. If I sit here under this sun much longer I'll go mad, and poor fair-skinned Bith hasn't been above deck in two days now and she still looks like a boiled lobster."

"You should see yourself, Cal," Bith shot back petulantly. "A scarecrow looks livelier than you right now."

"Thank the gods it is later in the season. I've heard tell that in winter ice forms on the sail-spars a half a foot thick, the deck is a slippery frozen terror, and the wind, the wind is a devil driving hail and sleet before it."

"Where they have taken Hathor it is winter," Endril said quietly, bringing idle conversation to a halt and returning them instantly to a sense of seriousness and purpose, as only sharp-tongued Endril could.

"I ask you, did he fight valiantly?" Cal praised his lost comrade rhetorically. "I flinch myself when I see that up-raised chopper!"

"We should have known. We should have formed the triangle and one, with Hathor at our center, to protect him. We knew it was him they were after," Bith berated herself and the other two.

"From the center he can't get full leverage with that weapon of his. We wouldn't have been nearly as effective. And anyway, we were greatly outnumbered. We did the best we could, and we are lucky to get away with our lives and the lives of these hundred-odd villagers," Endril pointed out, gesturing with a slight nod to the stern of the boat where a dozen or so of the townspeople lay dozing in the stultifying, windless heat of the day.

"What are we to do about them?" Cal asked quietly, and

Bith, straining to hear him, popped open a hatch cover and poked her head up to join the conversation.

"They are certainly our responsibility now. Their best man, the leader of the revolt, was killed in the skirmish at Steadfast-by-Sea. I believe his name was Hereric."

"I saw him die. Threnod himself stabbed him in the back while he fought with two of the lord's guards." Cal recounted this in plain, soldierly fashion, as if he were giving a report, but Endril and Bith could hear the suppressed anger in his voice.

"If we returned to our own lands now we could resettle them there, but that would delay us considerably, and every day that Hathor remains in the enemy's hands furthers their evil designs. Threnod is only a crass merchant, of that much I am sure. His intent was to sell the poor fellow. So haste is essential, if we are to follow Hathor." Endril neatly summed up the situation for the other two.

"What do you suggest we do?" Bith asked the elf, who would never come out and say what he really meant unless you asked him, preferring insult and innuendo.

"First, we must ask the people what it is they want."

"I already know the answer to that," Cal rejoined. "They want to go back to their homes."

"Impossible, at this time, don't you think?" said Endril. "Steadfast-by-Sea is a formidable stronghold. Even with the benefit of surprise, I'm not sure we could defeat Lord Threnod's forces."

"Suppose they weren't inside?" Bith asked innocently.

"Yes, that might work," Endril answered quickly, but Cal didn't understand the cryptic dialogue between them.

"What are you talking about?" he demanded to know. "I studied their fortifications while we were there. Lord Threnod may be a glutton and a coward, but he knows how to man a defensive perimeter and set up a chain of command."

"Steadfast-by-Sea is a fine fort, but it has one weakness.

To defend it one must be inside it, because it holds all the high ground."

"I still don't understand."

"Never mind for now. Bith has convinced me with one short question that we could topple Lord Threnod, if the villagers will fight again."

"Let's ask them."

The fishermen had a marvelous way of communicating between boats, which was often important as they worked together to drive schools of fish into their nets. By a combination of whistles and short sharp hand signals they were able to convey complex messages across wide stretches of water. The adventurers had seen the fisherfolk use it to keep each other in sight during the first wild moments of Bith's hurricane.

"If it's too foggy we can make do with whistles alone," one of the fishermen in the boat with them had said. "And if the wind is too noisy, hand-talk alone will do, but it's faster and easier to use them together."

Thus without having to bring the scattered fleet together or send dories between the vessels, they were able to hold a meeting and explain their proposal. Endril told the group aboard their boat that the three of them wanted to return to the village and counterattack. The signaler then conveyed the substance of Endril's speech to the dozen or so other boats in the fleet floating nearby in the calm waters. When the townspeople learned what was being proposed, they were less enthusiastic than Cal had predicted.

"If our leader Hereric were still alive, we might be brave enough to try it. But he is gone, and you too have lost your best warrior," the message came back and was assented to by the small group on board their boat. Cal resented the implication. He turned to his companions.

"In terms of pure strength and ferocity, yes, Hathor was our best, and we want to rescue him, but the three of us are still a formidable force. Tell them," he addressed the signalman, "tell them they must fight this battle for Hereric, in remembrance of his courage; that he would not want them to give up meekly upon his death, that to do so bespoils his honored memory. Whistle them that!" He finished with a shout, and the fisherman gestured and trilled energetically across the watery distance.

The answer came back not in whistles but in a faint cheer raised from all the boats. At first Cal thought they were cheering for his rousing speech, but then he saw men scurrying to hoist sails aloft on the other boats, and soon similar activity broke out on their boat. Across the water he could see a fluttering and stirring as myriad ripples breaking the smoothness of the water some distance away moved toward them.

"What is it? What's happening?" Bith asked, for she had missed the signs.

"We've won them over. Or rather, luck has swayed them. They have taken it as an omen that Cal raised the wind with his battle cry on Hereric's valor. Now we must hope our plan will work."

In a few minutes the fleet was under sail, a dozen billowing sheets swelling and flapping in the breeze, halyards clanking against their masts, and prows leaping forward, slicing through the waves. After so many hours without making headway, the sudden sensation of movement was a joy in itself. Cal raced to the bow of the boat, exulting in the race, urging the crew to pull out ahead of the other boats.

"Come on, lads, let's show 'em. Let's be the first to sight land, what do you say?"

Endril had proposed that they circle round and reach land to the south of the village, behind the jutting arm of the cove where the tide ran swift, but the villagers convinced him that the water was too shallow there. He learned that there was a second, smaller cove, uninhabited for lack of a freshwater source, just a few miles to the north of the village, so it was decided to circle north instead, and run in beneath the cover of darkness. As they were still more than two days' sail from port, there was plenty of time for Cal to give some classes in close-quarter fighting, which were piped and waved to the other boats in the same fashion. Bith made busy with preparations of her own that she would not reveal to Cal no matter how much he badgered her. Endril sat quietly, rubbing a flint against the murderous tips of each of his arrows until they were all hawk's-talon sharp and barbed. The villagers, initially skeptical and hesitant, grew more spirited as they approached their homeland, though Cal couldn't see how they told this patch of chilly water from that one, as they were still miles from a landfall. Rough, hardy folk, they proved to be decent fighters when given a little training. In addition to Samish, two brothers—the lean and muscled Sheerstrake and his stockier, bulkier brother Valdspar—stood out as valiant warriors. Cal appointed them as trainers and sent them to the other boats by dinghy to continue the training. On his own vessel Cal watched approvingly as the battling mariners practiced his maneuvers, and declared that Lord Threnod's men would have a harder time scattering them in a panic this go-around. Once during a session a sailor got so excited he threw his mock foe overboard in his fervent attempt to duplicate a hold Cal was demonstrating. Instead of reprimanding the man for the delay caused by having to rescue the victim (hurriedly—a few minutes in these icy waters and any man would perish), Cal praised him for his zeal.

"That's what a fight is—you must lose your head to save it, fight in a frenzy but be aware of what's around you, don't stampede, look for your fellow and protect his back while he defends yours. There'll be smoke and noise and men running this way and that and the cries of the wounded and the screams of the dying, but you must think only of the enemy—where is he, what is he doing? How can I get the advantage of him? And when you engage, don't think at all, just act and react, until you or he is still. Harsh, but that's the way it is."

"What about the womenfolk and the little ones?" Samish,

Hereric's brother and the de facto leader since his kinsman's death, asked Cal.

"They remain in the boats with a small guard, very small, since we need almost every man for the battle."

"If need be, they can sail these boats away from danger," Samish informed him.

"We can outsail the men, and outfish them too, if given the chance," one of the fishermen's wives spoke up.

"Fine, fine. We will time the attack for the deep of night, when the heaviest sleep is upon them, just after the change of guards when the new sentries are not yet accustomed to seeing in the dark," Cal said, describing what he thought to be a good plan. Bith, standing by and watching the instruction, shook her head but said nothing, and Endril smiled amusedly.

"You disapprove of the timing of the attack?" Cal challenged Bith, but she would not take the bait and divulge her intentions.

"Scheme on, my ambitious general," she teased him good-naturedly, and Cal, red-faced, ran the fishermen through another strenuous set of military exercises.

The wind remained fair and full behind them. They made good progress and soon approached the shore. The sighting of land brought a cheer that carried across the waves from boat to boat, heartening the dispossessed villagers with the thought that they might regain what was rightfully theirs. For Bith, Cal, and Endril, it was the idea that they might be able to find their missing fourth that pulled them toward shore and a certain battle with the well-trained soldiers of Lord Threnod. Having lost once already, and then with Hathor at their side, the three could not help but wonder if even with Bith's cunning and Cal's leadership and Endril's telling arrows they could prevail. Cal voiced his uncertainty as the sun went down on the last evening before they would strike land and establish a beachhead north of Steadfast-by-Sea.

"Suppose we can't dislodge them," he asked aloud as the three of them sipped from mugs of hot birchbark tea in the forward section of their boat, off away from the resting villagers. "What is this grand plan of yours, anyway, Bith?"

Coy Bith still refused to disclose her method for luring Lord Threnod's men from their castle, saying that her plan depended on absolute surprise.

"On our solemn oath, I won't tell a soul," Cal insisted, but Bith was adamant.

"If I told you, you probably wouldn't let me do it anyway," she added, which troubled Cal greatly, as in the absence of Hathor he felt even more strongly protective of the slender, soon-to-be-beautiful princess than ever before.

"If it's dangerous, don't do it."

"Of course it's dangerous, but no more so than grabbing the Runesword was for you or escaping Schlein's prison was for Endril."

"I won't have you risking your neck for me, it's not—not proper!" Cal sputtered, but Endril corrected him.

"We are all equal under the oath. That Bith is a woman is less important now than that she is one of us, dedicated to destroying the evil of the Mistwall and restoring our lands to bloom and vigor. Let us not forget the high purpose that first brought us north."

"Agreed," Cal admitted reluctantly, "but, Bith, remember, I am heading up this detachment. If I say jump, don't ask when or why, just jump!"

"Why?" Bith teased, but Cal would only repeat his last words: "Just jump!"

By good fortune the breeze brought with it a cloud-bank that gave the fleet cover to cross the last few miles to shore under the lowering vapors. An incoming tide also favored them, lifting the prows of the boats over the breakers and depositing them gently on the gravelly shore. Valdspar and Sheerstrake leapt out first. Quickly and quietly the seamen dragged their craft higher up on the beach and secured them with clever anchors of forged iron hooks on chains. A circular encampment was formed and lookouts posted. The villagers then surprised the three outcasts by revealing a secret of their own—before a battle they daubed themselves with paint beneath their eyes to give themselves a more fearsome aspect to their enemies.

"Why didn't you do this the first time you took on Lord Threnod's men, when you came to our rescue?" Cal asked Samish as he watched the headman applying the black goo, which came from the underbelly sac of one of the strange sea creatures they harvested, while Sheerstrake and Valdspar quietly sharpened the points of their wickedly barbed harpoons for the thousandth time.

"No time. We heard the skirmish and joined in. Had we prepared, the fight might ha' been over already."

Cal didn't know if Samish meant by this that the fight would have ended with the deaths of the three adventurers, or whether he meant that had they taken the time to prepare themselves ceremonially as they did now, they would have defeated Lord Threnod's men. He hoped it was the latter. Certainly the villagers did look like a changed lot, each with eyes blacked, a device that served both as camouflage and to increase the ferocity of each inflamed visage. There is no stronger motive in the world than fighting for your own land, save defending one's family. Often the two causes are warped and woven into one and the same cloth, as was the case tonight, for by bringing their families back to shore the seafaring men of the town risked losing all. But far worse for them would have been the wearying task of finding or fighting their way onto a new homeland, for it seemed that races of men lived anywhere there was good land to sow, or rich sea banks to fish, no matter how remote. Likely they would have been shipwrecked on some waterless barren rocky isle, or fallen prey to piratical bands that roamed the coastline and had once even attacked their village, or subjugated by some other lord even more powerful and brutal than Lord Threnod. No, they had made the right choice, for there was no place that man would be safe from man, and at least in Steadfast-by-Sea they knew their enemy and were not facing the unknown, and they were returning to contest what was theirs!

The women prepared a cold meal of salted meat and tough hard crackers, as it was too dangerous to light fires. Cal went among the men, finally able to talk to some of them face-to-face for the first time. He had grown weary and impatient of the seamen's ingenious seagoing communication system, but as he talked with them he realized that it had served its purpose, that these rugged men had picked up the training and would fight well for him. He complimented Samish on their readiness and fierce bearing.

"Life at sea toughens a man," Samish answered, and a woman slicing cold meat nearby overheard him and added:

"Life waiting for a man at sea toughens a woman."

Neither Cal nor Samish disputed her—both knew that it was better (and easier) to act than to wait—at least then one was doing something. Tonight everyone would play an active part, even those who stayed behind to guard the boats, for if the castle attackers were defeated, the boats would be their only hope to avoid slaughter, and those at the boats would have to be ready to launch them in an instant, or perish in a bloodbath at the hands of the castle's defenders.

In a show of solidarity, Cal blacked under his eyes too with the inky substance, but Bith and Endril declined to follow suit. Endril was unusually taciturn—perhaps he foresaw the difficult task before them more clearly than his ardent companion.

"They won't all come out, some will be too smart, and Lord Threnod will bully others, no matter how convincing Bith is," he declared morosely.

"All we need is an open gate or postern, and my fighters will handle the rest," Cal boasted. Endril shook his head in disagreement, but he didn't want to shatter the fragile confidence of the villagers in their combat abilities, so he said nothing.

At midnight a column moved out from the beach camp.

Instead of the usual cheering and singing of war songs that might accompany such a march in daytime, a pall of silence hung over the shuffling line of men, their voices hushed and their weapons muffled by cloth wrappings. Nary a torch lit their way, but this was the home turf of the men in the file, many of whom had never been farther away from Steadfast-by-Sea than Bith's storm had carried them. Their own feet had worn the path they walked upon now, and the sandy soil near the water crunched familiarly under them.

Lord Threnod was an outsider—he and his kin had arrived only a score of years before, at that time the first outsiders the villagers had ever seen. It did not take long for the ruthless lord to exert dominance over them, for they had suffered no previous invasions. Since that time the sea pirates had come and gone (Lord Threnod had barred the doors to Steadfast-by-Sea and left the villagers to the knives and long swords of the pirates—what was he himself but a pirate who had stayed—adding another grudge to the list of owed vengeances the seamen and their families held against him). Now, at last, under the leadership of an outsider, to be sure, but a good and mighty soldier with two magical allies, they would have an opportunity to seek long-awaited reprisal for years of cruel vassalage.

Barely able to contain his exhilaration, Cal raced back and forth along the edge of the strung-out line of men. After all, this would be his first real command. Bith and Endril had let him take charge for once, while they conspired over her plan at the rearguard position. He tried to remember his father's manner of leadership, not trying to make men like him, only to make them believe in him, to fight for him and his cause. This night of course that was no problem, as he and his friends had taken on the villagers' crusade.

Only a cursory patrol paced the forest's edge where the trees gave way to that sweeping lawn that ran to the sea. They easily overpowered this lax force. Cal personally took out the first one, running the haft in after the blade to prevent a gush of blood that could be spotted from a distance. He

dragged the fallen sentinel into the woods and waited for
the guard's partner to make his turn and head back this way,
but the man never came back. Samish had gutted him soundlessly as if he were a fresh fish. There remained, as they all
knew there would, the fifty or so yards of open ground,
sloping up to the walls. A mad charge across this stretch
would be suicidal. Back at camp Cal had thought to try
diversionary tactics so that he could run hastily constructed
ladders up under the walls if Bith's plan failed, but as he
stood before that sweep of barren terrain he realized that
everything depended on her ability to trick Lord Threnod's
men into coming out into the open. Bereft of cover, they
were at the mercy of the defenders in the turrets and along
the walls above.

Cal turned to look for Bith, but she was nowhere in the
darkness behind him. He gestured for Samish and his men
to spread out, but not too far, at the edge of the trees along
the front perimeter of the castle. Suddenly Endril was at his
elbow, pinching him.

"Be ready," the elf whispered, "and don't look too closely!"

While Cal wondered what in the gods' garden Endril was
talking about, his attention was suddenly attracted to two
swirling flames of light, circling about each other in the
underbrush. He cursed whoever had lost them the element
of surprise, for immediately a shout went up from atop the
long front wall of Steadfast-by-Sea, and a row of soldiers
lined the shooting stations, each position marked by a notch
in the wall.

The twin flares danced in motion forward out of the forest, and in the flickering trails of light Cal saw Bith, a flaming torch in each hand, dancing naked toward the castle gate. For a moment the young squire lost his soldierly
composure, as the sight of her pale, nubile, and lithe body
stunned him to inaction. Then Bith began to sing, not in a
quavery voice as when the Claviger had possessed her, but
in her own sweet adolescent tones, not singing really, but

babbling singsong like a person who has lost her mind.

"Who will have me? Who will take this virgin princess? I thirst! I hunger! I perish! I die! Shipwrecked, I have wandered for days in the forest, with cockleshells in my hair and dead men's eyes in my eyes, for I saw them floating down but their hair streamed up!" she rambled, still sweeping the two brands around and around her and dancing ever closer to the gate. Once Cal overcame the shock of seeing Bith in the nude, he quickly realized her crafty and cunning design. If Lord Threnod's men thought she was demented, they would consider her harmless and open their gates to bring her inside. Lord Threnod would no doubt like to sell her to flesh traders, perhaps the same ones who had purchased Hathor. Would it work? Bith was nearly to the gate. The soldiers on the upper wall whistled and cheered lewdly at her show, but none left their posts. Lord Threnod was nowhere in sight. At the gate, Bith stopped. She held the two flames away from her, arms extended straight out from her sides, in a gesture of invitation.

"Are none of you man enough for me? Is my royal blood too rich for you? Is there no prince among you? Cowards! Impotent eunuchs! I leave you then!" She turned and began to walk away with a provocative sway that brought a groan from the leering soldiers on the parapets. Cal and his men waited silently in the forest's fringe. Then the gate shuddered and opened with a scraping creak and Lord Threnod himself emerged, half-clothed, with a barbarous, lecherous gleam in his eyes.

"Ho ho, my young pretty princess, so the storm got you and your companions after all," he called after her, but Bith maintained her slow steady gait toward the woods. A few of Threnod's guards accompanied him, lagging just behind, and others waited at the gate. But they did not suspect the sudden murderous attack of the villagers, as Cal suddenly darted from the woods and clasped unclothed Bith to him for one sweet instant before nearly hurling her into the brush behind him so that he could face Lord Threnod.

"Draw your sword, for I'll not run you through from the back as you did poor Hereric!" Cal shouted, as his men, brave Valdspar and mighty Sheerstrake at their head, poured from their hiding places into the clearing and engaged Threnod's guards in a dozen scattered fights. A group of them prevented the closure of the gate by a heroic charge that cost several their lives. Cal and Lord Threnod dueled at close quarters, wailing and flailing their swords at each other. Out of the corner of one eye Cal saw Endril, perched on a low tree bough, carefully and accurately picking off key fighters in the fray with his slim bow.

Bith's plan worked brilliantly. The archers on the parapets above could not fire for fear of slaying their leader, nor could the spearmen hurl their weapons. They ran from their assigned spots to join the melee below, thus giving up the high ground. A battle is always chaotic, especially a night fight. The cloud-bank that had provided the fleet with cover to land now obscured the moon and stars, rendering torches along the castle wall as the only light. Bith reappeared in Cal's sight, dressed for battle and wielding a fish-cutter's knife with proficiency. The mock madness was gone from her eyes, replaced by determination. Heartened, Cal redoubled his efforts to overcome Lord Threnod, who proved to be less timid with a sword than Cal had expected. The breakthrough came when a second set of villagers, who hadn't reached the ships but had survived by hiding in the forest, joined the fray, bursting into the clearing in a crazed rush. They tumbled randomly into fighters, and their momentum carried the battle into the inner courtyard, separating Cal from his ungainly adversary in the confusion. Once inside, Cal's men quickly gained the advantage by sheer numbers and the passion of fighting for their homeland against the mercenaries of Lord Threnod. Some of them broke and ran outside the gate, leaving a smaller force within the walls. While the contest there raged on, the mercenaries regrouped and tried to retake the building, but the perimeter of Steadfast-by-Sea was protected by a glacis, a slope at the base of the wall to discourage the use of battering rams. This tilty bank made it difficult for scaling ladders to gain purchase as well. The villagers now held the high ground and the upper hand. Under Cal's barked orders, they secured all sides of the castle and posted guards along every wall.

Cal discovered the cell Hathor had been imprisoned in, and utilized the slit holes in the floor by raining down a volley of arrow shots, using the bow with both the left and the right hand, that scattered a breaching party. After repelling the counterattack, Cal raced around the parapet walk, searching for Threnod, but he had disappeared. Perhaps he had escaped with his paid soldiers, for he hadn't been among the counterattackers. The wounded on both sides were laid out in the courtyard, while the few of Threnod's men who remained were led to dungeon cells.

The three adventurers met up in the torch-lit courtyard, amid the groans of the wounded. "No sign of Hathor, but I could tell where they kept him, from the smell," Cal reported.

"You didn't expect him to be here, did you?" Endril asked caustically. As he spoke, he was rubbing a strange ointment on a skinned elbow, the only scratch suffered by any of the three.

"What is that salve?" Bith asked, as she was always interested in new potions and lotions.

"Ground-up fish scales mixed with tincture of antimony," Endril replied. "A villager showed it to me. Apparently something in the fish is good for healing cuts."

"That was quite a show you put on." Cal laughed. "You sure had them going up on the wall. But every second you were out there I waited for the fatal arrow to pierce you."

"As did I, my hero, as did I. I couldn't think of another way to get them out."

"Had they caught you, an arrow wouldn't have been the only thing to—" Endril started to say, but a loud groan from the well at the center of the courtyard drew his attention. The three adventurers raced to the well head and discovered

Lord Threnod, halfway down, wedged into the cavity by his flabby bulk.

"Come out of there, you fat old lech, or there'll be no water to drink."

"I'm stuck," came the miserable reply.

"Then we'll hoist you out like a cow that stumbled into a sinkhole. Catch this!" Cal shouted, and he tossed the well bucket and its attached rope down onto Lord Threnod's head. The half-filled pail emptied its contents on the way down and doused the fallen lord, and the vessel rattled off his head.

Amid much merriment from the assembled villagers Lord Threnod was raised in herks and jerks from his ignominious resting place. Finally he tumbled over the rim of the well and lay gasping at their feet. At the sight of him the mood of the mob turned angry and Cal had to stand between them and the humiliated lord to prevent immediate violence. Some wanted to paint him with hot tar, others proposed a tug-of-war with his limbs, and some already had their filleting knives out and were sharpening them against their leather belts.

"Men! People!" Cal shouted. "You must not act out your vengeance on this sorry fool! To do so is to become like him. Instead I propose that he be put on the lowliest work detail, when you use the prisoners to rebuild the houses and shops and outbuildings his men destroyed."

A cheer went up. The townspeople liked Cal's plan. In addition to being just, it also prolonged their opportunity for revenge. After all, they had been under his thumb for many years now. Why should he get away with a quick slitting of his throat? No, let him carry out the wet ashes of their clothes and their furniture from their burnt homes. They would outfit themselves from the stores of Steadfast-by-Sea, which Threnod had accumulated by appropriating the fruits of their work and sweat.

Twenty or so of the hundred-odd townsmen, including intrepid Valdspar and staunch Sheerstrake, volunteered to sail north with Bith, Cal, and Endril in search of Hathor. Despite threats of torture Lord Threnod would admit only that Hathor was taken in that direction, which they had already surmised from earlier events. Evidently Lord Threnod feared whomever he had sold Hathor to more than Cal, whose heart was not in the prospect of hurting anyone except in a fair fight. Inflicting pain on an unresisting victim had no appeal for him, much as it would have satisfied the cravings of the townsmen for hurtful revenge.

"I'd strangle the bastard with my bare hands if that would help, but he quivers at the prospect not of strangulation but of what his client might do to him if he confessed. Strange, that the unseen menace is worse than the known one."

"Not really," Endril commented. "You humans always have such fancies. You always make the imagined terror worse than the reality," he ended with a sardonic laugh.

"Not in this case, perhaps," Cal said. "Until we know what sort of foe we have, it is better to overestimate the enemy's strength than underestimate it. This is one of the first laws of combat."

"Agreed," Endril responded, surprising Cal. Bith nodded her head vigorously in assent.

"We sail in the morning, then?" she wanted to know.

"Why wait?" Cal asked.

"Agreed again," Endril pitched in, suddenly compliant. "We are already a week behind, but we'll make some of that up by sailing instead of crossing the great northern plain, though we'll have to hike inland to the west at some point."

"Do you know where we're going, then?"

"Where we were always going—Dripping Hall in the land of the Wind-Websters."

"How did you figure that out, elf?"

"What makes you think Hathor will be there?" Bith inquired. "Lord Threnod denied that he had sold Hathor to them when we asked him about it."

"Lord Threnod told a half truth," Endril countered. "Half truths are half lies. He didn't say Hathor wouldn't be there, only that he hadn't sold him to the Wind-Websters. I believe there was an intermediary, who is perhaps the real foe and the evil behind the rent in the Mistwall, but our best hope is to intercede at the break point. Hathor will be there, I am sure. In what condition he will be, I cannot say."

"We sail tomorrow," Cal said grimly, and the three weary but victorious fighters retired for a well-deserved night's rest, while in the courtyard of Steadfast-by-Sea the ecstatic villagers celebrated their return, their victory, and their freedom with songs and feasting.

CHAPTER
10

Hathor's trip from the mountaintop castle of the Queen of Ice to Dripping Hall took only three days. Hathor was allowed to ride standing up in the back of an ox-cart rather than being caged up in the boxy wagon in which he had been brought from Steadfast-by-Sea. He did not see the queen again before he was lashed to the front crosspiece of the cart and led out of camp behind a deaf old bull that had also lost its sense of smell and did not react to Hathor's presence at all. To the ox, Hathor was merely another heavy load, another burden to bear. Hathor spoke to the beast in its own language, but the animal was truly hard of hearing and ignored him. Thrydwulf had slipped Hathor a shaggy blanket that he wrapped round himself, so that he looked like one of the forlorn dancing bears he had seen at village carnivals, mangy and dispirited beasts dismally waiting their turn to prance for coins for their master and perhaps a crust of bread for themselves.

Hathor dimly remembered from Endril that "webster" meant "weaver." *But how does one weave the wind?* Hathor wondered. He soon found out. Crossing west, Hathor and

115

the contingent of guards escorting him passed through foot-hills like those to the east. When they emerged onto the western valley floor, they entered another frozen waste like the northern plain but dotted here and there by surprising patches of green. Standing like sentinels above each of these stretches of farmland was a whirling set of blades mounted to a tower, endlessly turning in the stiff breeze that raced out of the mountains toward the south. The landscape was dotted with these combinations of whirring wind-looms and their plots of green amid the general desolation.

What do they do? Hathor pondered the mystery and scratched his heavy head. He had never seen the like of it. From a distance he could hear the creaking of the wooden paddles as they went round, almost scraping the ground as they passed low, then reaching above the top of the tower, fifty feet and more high up at their peak. To Hathor they looked like giant's toys. He could see no visible purpose to the turning. He asked a guard about it, but none of them was as friendly as Thrydwulf, and they wouldn't give him an answer. Then in an instant of discovery he figured it out for himself. As a cave-dweller, he knew that there was water deep beneath the earth, the purest, softest, sweetest water trapped for who knows how long in underground reservoirs. Cave tunnels often led down to these pools, submerged in darkness. But even here, Hathor realized, in this cold desert, there must be water underground. The wind-looms were like great well buckets, plunging down to fetch up the water from below. From water came green plants and food. Any fool knew that. It was so obvious. Pleased with himself, Hathor looked at the steeples and their rotating arms with new curiosity. He noticed that in places they were lined up in rows along raised embankments, like soldiers in a column, the better to catch the wind. When he arrived at the first of these spectacular structures, he discovered that the Wind-Websters had put the wind-looms to another amazing use. The blades caught wind, spun the wheel, and dredged the water, true enough. But in addition, the turning wheel stored up its energy by winding taut a coil of thick rope on a wooden spool and by raising a counterweight. When the rope was unwound and the counterweight lowered, it turned other pulleys connected to stones that ground grain, paddles that churned butter, and other devices. Hathor could see that even after the wind dropped, the stored-up tension would allow work to continue until the counterweight was fully lowered and the cable completely unwound. Such mechanisms were like a form of magic to Hathor.

Off in the distance, almost at the edge of the horizon, was the Mistwall. Hathor had never seen it this far north. Here it took on some of the shimmery, luminous qualities of the Northern Lights. It seemed less dangerous, but that was an illusion. At the rip, visible even from a distance, frosty exhalations of cold air swirled and billowed, as though pressure was building up that would soon open a vaster hole. It was clear to Hathor now why the Queen of Ice was in league with the Wind-Websters. With their powerful wind-looms, they could blow the northern air southward in great quantities, expanding her frigid demesne. The cold wind would be more productive in their looms, turning them faster, but Hathor doubted the Wind-Websters comprehended the queen's evil motive, her desire to turn the whole world into an ice-capped desert. He, Hathor, was the only one who knew the full madness of her evil intent. What disaster lay ahead if she succeeded in ripping open the Mistwall and cascading cold weather down upon the peoples of the south!—and he was a prisoner—he could do nothing to stop her.

Hathor stretched and tested the hemp bonds that tied his hands to the ox-cart, as he had done several times a day since the beginning of the trip. His legs were still in irons, so there was no thought of running away, but if he could free his hands for a minute he might be able to do some damage. But the hemp was treated with a toughening liquid that made it impossible for Hathor to burst apart the rope or chew through it. The entourage entered the region of the wind-looms with Hathor still firmly imprisoned. Each family, it seemed, owned one or more of the immense towers, which were vaguely pyramidal in shape, each with a cross of wind-blades affixed to its windward side. Workers tended the various pulley-driven devices that ran off the power of the wind-looms. When the cart containing Hathor rumbled by, they looked up disinterestedly. Hathor saw that many (though not all) were non-humans like himself, ogres or trolls or orcs. They were slaves! The humans among them were rough-looking, criminal types, with faces more grotesque than the ugliest orc's. All worked tirelessly under the watchful supervision of Wind-Websters. The first one Hathor ever saw—a tall, graceful-looking human with bland features except for whitish hair much fairer than his own—was lashing an orc with a whip. Hathor could not tell what the poor creature's sin had been, but the punishment was savage and relentless, the Wind-Webster following the orc as it crawled away, badly beaten, in order to administer one more welt-raising blow. Walking away, the Webster laughed. Hathor growled from his position in the cart. The Webster jumped back, startled. When he saw the source of the snarl, however, a cruel expression masked itself over his innocuous countenance. He strode to the cart and paced alongside, prodding Hathor with the butt end of the whip.

"Is it for sale?" he asked one of the guards, and when the reply came back in the negative, he spat and said: "Pity. With a little whipping this one could do some work, no doubt." He raised his whip to strike and Hathor cringed before the expected blow, but one of the guards placed a lance between him and the Webster, saying:

"This one goes to the palace. He can't be harmed."

The Webster backed away immediately. "They always take the best for themselves, men, women, and—whatever that is!" he said with another cold laugh, pointing at Hathor. Dropping off to return to his creaking loom, he examined Hathor again, and though covered by the hairy blanket, Hathor felt exposed before the Wind-Webster's cool gaze.

Each succeeding Wind-Webster he saw looked remarkably like the first, a whole race of rangy white-haired humans of vacuous visages, all busily tending their little plots and their clever wooden machines.

At the center of the valley was a palace built like a giant replica of the other wind-looms, except that it had no blades, for they would have had to have been hundreds of feet long and were beyond the ability even of these clever people. Ten or so smaller towers were clustered round it like goslings round a goose, providing the larger edifice with water and water-driven power. The road they traveled grew more crowded as they approached the castle, with carts and wagons carrying local produce to market, and other wagonloads of slave workers like Hathor, jammed ten and twelve to a cart where Hathor rode alone. A line of them waited at the palace gate to be passed by the guards there. Hathor peered into the wagon next to him and saw among others a female troll, stout and mottle-skinned, waiting with bowed head to be brought in for assignment.

Hathor caught her attention and asked her where she came from, but she only looked at him with dull eyes and said: "Does it matter?" and then after a minute she added: "You work until you die here. It doesn't take long—" Then her cart started up again and soon vanished into the confines of the palace. Hathor's cart soon followed under the daub and wattle wall, which didn't look very strong to Hathor until he saw the outlines of foot-thick beams beneath the smooth plaster. This wall ran unbroken round the main tower, leaving an open ring between it and the inner tower wall, where much of the daily life of the palace occurred. People milled about, passing to and fro with apparent purpose amid the hubbub, though to Hathor it seemed like chaos itself had descended. To protect against attack, the main gate to the inner tower was not in a line with the outer gate but instead was set off to one side, so that invading parties would have to fight their way along the circular corridor before breaching the inner citadel. Since Hathor had met

Lord Threnod and the Queen of Ice, he expected to be taken before the leader of the Wind-Websters, whose name he had not even heard yet, but instead his wagon was pulled from the line at the inner gate by the palace quartermaster, an officious and impatient Webster with a mild grimace permanently affixed to his otherwise uninteresting face.

"Ah! The new troll! Excellent! Today is market day. You can start immediately. Come, come! Off with that gross cover. You'll work up a sweat in no time. Out there!" Hathor's blanket was taken from him. The queen's guard was dismissed. He was shoved and tugged by his new captor through a narrow tunnel in the wall of the tower. Momentarily he was inside the palace itself, but they traveled quickly down a side hallway and before Hathor's eyes could adjust to the sudden darkness they passed through the wall again out to a bustling outdoor marketplace built against another part of the wall, with thirty or forty stalls lining the curving foundation of the tower, each a tent or lean-to and each with a merchant hawking wares and a small crowd gathered round. They had taken a shortcut directly through the palace, Hathor realized vaguely, so as not to walk around the enormous loop of the tower's base. The beadle hustled Hathor along until they reached a stall containing a menagerie of animals, including squealing pigs, all manner of fowl, donsel-ewes with their peculiar purple fleece, wildly plumed pherassants, and even an ox and a couple of cows.

"Bludsoe. Here be your new butcher."

Butcher! Hathor thought, stunned by the idea. Since his conversion to vegetarianism, Hathor had found it difficult to kill even the leeches, tics, and mosquitoes that sucked his blood in the swamps near his home. To slaughter helpless, innocent creatures—no, he couldn't do it.

"No," he said, but already they were dragging him away from the cart, still bound by rope at the hands and by manacles on his feet. Bludsoe—a muscular, fleshy human with a florid red face bloated from drink, dressed in an unimaginably filthy and bloody leather apron—seized Hathor by bound wrists and dragged him bodily to his station, which was a wooden platform awash in entrails and gooey blackened drying blood.

"Wring their necks, drain their blood into that pail, and toss them into that basket. Got it?" The thuggish Bludsoe gave Hathor his orders as nonchalantly as if he were telling him to sweep the floor, not take the life of a hundred feathered friends. Hathor had always loved waterfowl, who inhabited the same sort of homeland as Hathor, at the edge of boggy lakes and slow-moving streams. Sometimes in wet weather they would nestle at the mouth of his cave, never coming all the way in but sharing the damp cover in a separate sort of way.

"My chains," Hathor pleaded, but Bludsoe, big and crude-looking as he was, would not chance Hathor escaping.

"You can work with the manacles on today. If you behave, we'll see about tomorrow. Now get started!" he snarled. Still bound hand and foot, Hathor stumbled onto the platform and looked before him. Lined up in rows were the stages of the execution: the pen of caged fowl, quacking and clicking their bills nervously, the half-filled pail of duck's blood, the basket of carcasses. Hathor could not bear to look in the bright, frenzied eyes of the captive birds.

"What's wrong with you? Get going!" Bludsoe cursed him and threatened him with a heavy stick. Resigned to his fate, Hathor withdrew a squawking bird from the cage awkwardly, because both hands were close together in their bindings, and when the bird nipped him with his bill, Hathor flinched and jerked and the bird went limp. He had killed it accidentally.

"Well done. Now slit its throat and empty its veins, and you're on to the next one," Bludsoe instructed him. Hathor stared at the lifeless form dangling from his clenched fists. He scarcely comprehended what he had just done.

"Fresh kill here!" Bludsoe shouted, but the crowd that gathered was there to see the new butcher, his anguished face streaming with tears, as one by one he slew the ducks and tossed them onto an ever-growing pile.

"Look! He cries! What's the matter, dainty?" a ribald wit shouted from the crowd. "Haven't you ever killed before?"

"And a troll for all that! Use those teeth!" another shouted, and the assembled crowd howled its pleasure at the spectacle of the whimpering Hathor at his work. Apparently the Wind-Websters gave no thought to killing animals, and found Hathor's sensitivity in the matter humorous. By the end of the day Hathor had emptied three cages of ducks and Bludsoe had sold them all to curious onlookers. Ordinarily Hathor was loathe to bathe more than once a fortnight, but this night he eagerly sought the cleansing water provided him by Bludsoe, and heaped great handfuls of it over his blood-specked form, washing himself repeatedly until Bludsoe dragged him away from the washtub. Bludsoe, as an indentured servant, was permitted a hovel outside the palace wall where he kept an ugly wife and several filthy urchins, but Hathor was securely chained to a corner post of the butchery where he slept his first night in Dripping Hall amid the ghastly remains of the day's killing and the squeals of frightened animals not yet led to slaughter.

Bludsoe was at first disgusted by the troll's sobs and moans, but he quickly realized that he would sell more and earn more as long as Hathor was his apprentice. And indeed, Hathor proved so popular an attraction he instantly became known as "the Weeping Butcher of Dripping Hall," because each day as he began his work he started to cry, and did not stop until he came down from the killing platform, and no amount of cursing and cajoling from Bludsoe could break him of his teary habit.

"The world must eat!" Bludsoe reminded him, but Hathor would have no discourse with him. Early on, Hathor had watched Bludsoe casually snap the back of a little porker, and in the knave's eyes he had seen a glint of perverse pleasure. From then on he refused to speak to his erstwhile master. And so the days went on for Hathor, a nightmare of blood and death without release. After three days he was removed (over loud protests from Bludsoe, who knew that he was losing both a good worker and a source of profit from the throngs he attracted) to the Royal Butchery, where hundreds often gathered to watch him, his eyes brimming and burning, as he plied his trade.

The Royal Butchery supplied the needs of the entire tower, all the courtiers and palace visitors, functionaries, the Royal Guard, and more. Oh, there was much butchering to be done, and a staff of knife-wielding aproned servitors to do the job. Hathor was now thoroughly inundated with blood and gore. He was forced to kill large animals, ox and woldebeast, sheep, deer, royal elk, and the like, in addition to myriad fowl, fish, and swine. Daily Hathor met and exceeded his quota of execution. By this time the bonds on his wrists had been removed to allow him to better employ his tools, but he remained manacled at the ankles, a terrible figure in the bloodstained smock he had been given to wear, steadily raising and felling his axe against unresisting necks and throats.

Hathor became strangely docile. He could no longer even muster a growl when the other butchers ganged up on him and gave him the worst jobs. The Royal Butchery was situated behind the palace near the livery stables. Several corrals and pens held quantities of animals in reserve, and new shipments arrived daily to supply the needs of the palace. Once the purveyors brought in the carcass of a whale dragged all the way from the Sea of Storms, a stinking, rotting cadaver forty feet long, its underbelly matted with grass and gravel rubbed into its skin during the long haul. The other butchers played a joke on Hathor. They put him inside the huge sea creature and told him to chop his way out, which he did, emerging from the blubbery interior gasping for breath and slimy with greasy innards. As if that wasn't enough, he then had to slice huge filets from the creature, cutting away the putrid portions of the flesh until he reached edible remains. Gagging and choking, Hathor stumbled among the slippery discarded whale bones and hunks of meat like one lost in a fog, his sorrow increasing with every hack he made into the dead beast's bulk. No sooner had he finished this grotesque chore than they ordered him to start in on a hairy ox that had been run over by a cart. His mangled twisted remains were brought in on the same cart, its bovine form scarcely recognizable.

The more he was asked to butcher, the quieter and more withdrawn Hathor became. He knew the desire of the Queen of Ice: that he slip and sink back down to the life he rose out of, that he become an ordinary cannibalistic troll again, killing and eating whatever came his way. He was determined not to let that happen. Only the chilly weather kept the stink in the butchery down to tolerable levels. The Wind-Websters were hearty meat-eaters despite their thin frames. They made use of almost all the edible portions of the animals they culled, even sweeping up the tangled entrails for sausage casings, and slicing up the organ meats for stuffing them. As for Hathor, he made do with a sparse diet of root vegetables and hard stale crackers while his greasy fellows feasted on broiled meats, one of the few advantages of the lowly butcher's job.

Among the other butchers were two smaller, younger trolls of a different clan than Hathor. He learned that they were brothers, torn from their mother's arms during a raid by Lord Threnod several years ago and sold directly to the Wind-Websters. They knew nothing of the Queen of Ice. When Hathor heard the name of his nemesis Threnod uttered, he felt a feeble spark of the old trollish anger, but quickly lapsed again into resigned apathy. He recalled the words of warning the female of his kind had spoken to him at the palace gate: "*You work until you die. It doesn't take long.*" Indeed, he had labored so hard and was fed so poorly that after a single week, while no one would ever mistake him for a Wind-Webster, his usually thick body showed its ribs and his blunt features became skull-like as his flesh receded. He settled into a pathetic routine—

up at dawn and work with silent sorrowful demeanor all day long, a single rudimentary meal in the early evening, and long hours of fitful, haunted sleep. Sometimes the deer he killed came back to him in nightmares, pleading to him with doe eyes for their innocent lives. In his sleep he petted them and released them, but then he would wake to another day of death blows.

Dripping Hall seemed an unlikely appellation for a land-locked palace that had to pump its water from below ground. One day Hathor overheard a beanpole-shaped Wind-Webster explaining to his equally lanky son how the place came to be called by that name. The story explained much more to Hathor than merely the palace's distinctive title. It seemed that once this valley had been a warm, verdant place, though how long ago that was no one could say. Then there had been no wind-looms, and no need for them, for plants grew everywhere amid the lushness of streams, fields, and meadows. The winters were mild, and the summers long and lazy. Then one year the snows did not melt after they fell, as they had previously. Instead they continued to blow down and build up drifts and sweep across the valley floor, day after day, long past the usual season for winter storms and much more severe than the ancestors of the Wind-Websters had ever experienced. At first they had no idea how to protect themselves against the elements. Many died of starvation because they were used to being able to grow crops year-round and had not stored away anything for the customarily short winters. Others went out in the suddenly fierce cold without proper coverings and froze in the biting wind. Still others wandered far from town in search of forgotten plants in the frozen ground and were lost in terrifying blizzards that turned the whole world white in their eyes.

As Hathor listened to the story, never ceasing from his gruesome tasks, he realized that he knew more about the tale than the Wind-Webster did—or more than he was telling his young son. Hathor knew where the invading cold came from, or, rather, from whom it was sent. The Wind-Webster gave his son an interesting but false account of the natural gradual changing of the weather. Hathor knew that what he was describing was the earliest employment of the Queen of Ice's power. In return for pledging eternal allegiance to her, the Wind-Websters saw the glacial air retreat, though not completely. The valley never returned to its original luxuriant state, but instead remained as it was today, a desolate place that was revived only by the clever workings of the Wind-Websters, whose ingenuity was inspired by hardship.

Why would the Wind-Webster lie to his son? Perhaps the shame of subjugation was too great to tell. Or perhaps the Wind-Websters had truly forgotten the real story, and now served the Queen of Ice only for profit, not remembering the tribulations she had inflicted on them.

Even in a prison or a butchery there must be moments of respite. For Hathor, his rest came after the slaughtering was finished for the day and before dreams came to torment his sleep. He hardly thought about his three companions anymore—they were either lying in watery sleep on the bottom of the Sea of Storms, or long since gone on to some other adventure, having forgotten about him. Who would look to rescue a smelly old troll, anyway? Even the Queen of Ice no longer seemed to care whether he lived or died. As long as he kept up his axe-wielding work in the butchery, he might go on forever, not really living but not yet dead, in a kind of shadowy, hellish half existence. He was like the Bog Man, Hathor realized with repugnance, except instead of being filled with preservative bog juice he was slowly being poisoned with his own indifference. The tears came less and less easily every day, and though he had been there just over a week it seemed to Hathor that he had known no other life but this one, that his other memories were merely good dreams to counter the fearful ones that played in his head all night, the ones where the animals begged him for mercy, and others in which they rose up against him, trampling him with cloven feet, shod feet, clawed feet, ripping at his flesh with fangs, talons, and nails. "Oh, woe! Oh, woe!" Hathor lamented, and to soothe himself in his brief moments of lull, he would sing to himself the lullaby his mother had sung him so many years ago:

Sleep baby troll in this warm hole,
The earth is your baby cradle.
The night is drear, but mother is here,
Sleep, sleep while you are able.

With this childhood song running round in his brain, Hathor would slip into a heavy, restless slumber where those terrifying visions lay in wait for him.

CHAPTER
11

It was dangerous to travel as the three adventurers and their tiny army of twenty were doing, in a large group in daylight. A lone traveler risked being assaulted by thieves. Three or four together ran the chance of being mistaken for thieves themselves. But a group of armed men could incur the wrath of every ruler in each region they passed through, and bring the full weight of a real army down upon them. Many an innocent party of voyagers had been wiped out to the last man when they were perceived as a marauding band by those whose territory they crossed. But really, they had no choice in the matter. The sea voyage north had consumed almost a full week. To pick their way at night through unknown terrain would simply take too long, especially for Cal, whose exhilarating victory at Steadfast-by-Sea had engendered in him a foolish recklessness that Endril was trying unsuccessfully to curb with sarcasm.

"One battle does not a war win," he chided Cal as they marched together across the northern edge of the tundral plain. By sailing north, they had eliminated the need to cross that bleak terrain. Now they marched due west toward Dripping Hall. Lord Threnod had been forced to detail its location to them before they left him in the hands of the villagers, though he seemed strangely eager to do so. Between them and the land of the Wind-Websters lay a range of icy mountains. None of the three had ever been to this remote area, nor had any of the villagers, but the seacoast people's folklore was replete with stories of the mountains' queen in her icy lair, and Endril secretly feared that this was the reason Threnod had been so willing to confide Dripping Hall's point on a map—he assumed they'd never reach their destination.

"You have cause for concern, elf. The cold may get to you, with that scrawny body of yours, but me, I like climbing mountains, it's invigorating."

"And what of this Ice Queen? Suppose she turns out to be more than mere legend?"

"It's Queen of Ice, not Ice Queen. And suppose she is real? We've handled worse."

"Threnod seemed to fear her, if indeed it was her whom he sold Hathor to."

"Threnod is a buffoon. But wait, I don't understand now. I thought you said it was the Wind-Websters. We never did get it out of him."

"No. And that's what worries me about how willing he was to place Dripping Hall for us. Perhaps he was lying. Perhaps this Queen of Ice is our real enemy. We know nothing about her, other than from myth and rumor. The Wind-Websters' fame had reached us in the south, along with news of the Mistwall, yet nothing was said of this other powerful personage. What does that tell you?"

Cal, irritated, played dumb. "I don't know, what?"

"That she is clever, secretive, and strong."

"If she exists at all."

"Oh, I believe she exists, alright, if only to put stumbling blocks in front of ardent youngsters like yourself. Why, two hundred years ago—" Endril began, but then he stopped.

They had reached the extreme edge of the plain. Just ahead they would enter the forest where Hathor had seen his first sleds and sled dogs. At the point where they would enter the forest, some miles east of where the party carrying Hathor had breached it, a lone, tall pine stood out from its brothers, a sole sentinel that seemed to have advanced some forty yards from the line of the forest to call attention to itself. The disused trail they followed took them directly by this unusual tree, and as they approached it while talking, sharp-eyed Endril had observed that a marker was affixed to its lower trunk, and when he was close enough to read it he interrupted himself in surprise.

"Well what do you know? A message from the very one we speak of."

Now all could read the large black letters scraped with charcoal from the end of a burnt stick on a white oak board in plain unvarnished language:

TURN BACK OR PERISH

"No risk of missing the meaning in those words, is there?" Cal joked, but he could see that the sign had its effect on the scarcely tested men of the village. It was one thing to fight and die for their land, and quite another to risk their lives in this forsaken north country on a mission to save a troll's life. Still, they owed these three strangers a great debt, and they had given their word. One could see it in the weather-beaten but still clear eyes of men like the brothers Valdspar and Sheerstrake. There was no more to say, they would go on without question, whatever lay ahead.

In a show of bravado, Cal ordered the company to camp under the signal pine, directly beneath the warning sign. It was a tricky maneuver that could have backfired, turning an already gloomy group even more somber, but this time it worked to Cal's advantage. As they sat around the tree, the men of the village became accustomed to the grim notice, and it lost some of its shock effect, as Cal had hoped.

"I think Bith may again prove the most effective of the three of us," Endril said as pointedly as his ears were pointed, which was significantly.

Cal munched on one of the last of Hathor's apples and spoke with his mouth full. "Why do you say that, elf?"

"The Queen of Ice is obviously some sort of demoness, not human or even witch or wizardess. She must be like unto a god or goddess, except that no one worships her, they only fear her. If she is from the world of demons, then Bith's magic may be our most useful weapon."

"No more displays like at Steadfast-by-Sea! I forbid it!" Cal shouted, to the amusement of his followers from the village, who secretly thought Cal a rather straitlaced lad, despite his noble valor. "The Young Shark," Valdspar called him.

"No. None of that. But it may be a severe test for her."

"Ha!" Cal said. "So far every time she uses magic it's overkill. Let's see what happens when she comes up against a real adversary."

"Remember, we are still without Hathor, our best fighter. Our success at Steadfast-by-Sea stemmed from the element of surprise we enjoyed. It is apparent"—Endril gestured to the foreboding sign, a dry tone to his voice—"that we have lost that advantage here."

"Alright then. When the moment comes, I'll let Bith step forward. Until then, however, we must maintain orderly march." He'd had the seafaring villagers practicing their drill step as they walked, until they longed for the rolling deck beneath their feet.

"Perhaps our best tactic would be to avoid the mountains and circle south," Bith suggested, but both Endril and Cal agreed that they had lost too much time already, that the mountain route was the most direct, that even if they managed to circumvent a confrontation with the Queen of Ice here, they would likely have to deal with her later, and that it was better to face their enemies separately rather than in league with each other.

"You talk about her now as if you were certain of her existence—I thought she was only *possibly* real," Bith pouted.

"Talking of her makes her come alive, it is so with all gods," Endril said wisely, but that bit of knowledge was beyond the understanding of his two young comrades. With that they broke camp and entered the forest, closing up rank to move in a tight defensive formation. As it was now two weeks since Hathor and his party had crossed this region, and thus a fortnight later in the season, the snowdrifts were even thicker, and without the benefit of dogs or sleds to break trail, the going was slow and strenuous. Endril and Bith were light enough that some of the time they were able to walk on the frozen crust, but Cal, weighted both by his chain mail and his muscular bulk, repeatedly broke through and floundered in the hip-deep snow, as did the villagers. At the end of the first day in the woods, they had journeyed barely two miles from the sentinel tree. Many more miles lay ahead to the first of the mountain cliffs. Huddled around a sweet popping pine-pitch fire that night, the three discussed their predicament.

Endril led off: "This is rough going. Perhaps Bith and I should venture ahead, as we make the fastest progress—"

"I'm against it," Cal, ever the military thinker, reasoned aloud. "We've already been split up by the loss of Hathor. To separate again would further dilute our strength. Give me a day to get used to the conditions and my speed will pick up."

"Not likely," said Endril. "If anything, you and your men will slow down as your thigh muscles grow weary from the unnatural effort of plunging through the stuff."

"Damn you, elf—" Cal flared, but Endril soothed him.

"I'm only being honest, Cal. Though we can see mountains, they are miles ahead and we don't know how far we have to travel to reach them, nor what we will find there when we do. Wouldn't it be better for us to explore ahead, at least search for the best route?"

"I'm still opposed." Secretly Cal feared most the thought of marching through the forest without the elf's wisdom and Bith's magic reserves at his side, but he would not admit that, even to himself. "Our strength is in unity," he said.

"Your men are not used to this footsore business of marching," Endril continued persuasively. "In their work they plant their feet on a pitching deck, not trudge and tread all day."

" 'Tis true, it's hard on them. But we can't go it alone, otherwise I'd send them back in an instant." Cal knew that the villagers, though game, were foot-weary. He also knew that good and loyal men that they were, they would not renege on a promise given in gratitude. He glanced at them, gathered around their own roaring fire just beyond the bent boughs of a sheltering pine. The cold would not affect this rugged breed, who had faced the teeth of winds howling out of the northeast to assail their boats upon the Sea of Storms, but their sealskin boots were inadequate for long marches. That was Cal's mistake, he should have noticed it, but what could he have done about it? Have new boots made? Not likely. Then Cal remembered a trick an old soldier had taught him for preserving his feet when his boots gave out. But it required cloth, a big sheet of cloth; what did he have that he could use? Suddenly he remembered—he had just the item! Quickly he opened his carry-sack and shoved an arm in and fished around blindly in his excitement. Yes, there it was, neatly rolled and stuffed in the bottom of the sack, his father's field pennant, the red eagle clutching its prey, blazoned on a field of green, that he had rescued from the Dark Army. Withdrawing the flag, Cal rose from his place with Bith and Endril and crossed to the villagers' fire as his two comrades watched silently, unsure of his intent. When he hesitantly ripped the flag into strips, Bith drew in her breath sharply, for she knew what a precious treasure it was to Cal and at what cost it had been lost and gained. *A leader must sacrifice for his troops,* was Cal's lofty unspoken reply to her sympathetic expression. He threw himself into the task, demonstrating the old soldier's technique of wrapping strips of cloth around his heels and under his soles to strengthen the boot in key places and provide some padding for the constant jarring of the march.

"This'll help you boys," he said. "I'm sorry it took me a day to think of it."

" 'Better now than after the tide's gone out,' " Sheerstrake replied, quoting an old seacoast adage.

The flag yielded a dozen or so strips, and from among the villagers enough cloth was found to outfit them all. That accomplished, Cal returned to Bith and Endril, who had watched the episode in silence. In his hands were the tattered remains of the flag, the last vestiges of a once-proud heritage, a bit of red talon, a ragged bit of green background. Cal tried not to show it, but there were tears in his eyes as he went to put the scraps in his sack.

"Give me those!" Bith ordered him. Cal stopped short in surprise. "Let me have them!" she commanded again, and Cal dumbly handed them over. "Now turn around, both of you!" Endril, not given to taking orders from anybody, blanched but obeyed, as did Cal. The two males heard some female mumbling behind them, then a sharp single curse, then silence. Then: "You can turn around now."

"What the—" Cal began, but then his jaw stopped working as he stared in amazement at the flag Bith held in her hands, completely restored in one piece, the glorious eagle again upswooping with clenched claws. "It's not perfect— I got mixed up a little—" Bith admitted, and Cal saw that, indeed, the flag was slightly smaller than he remembered, but it was a wonder that it was there at all.

"It's perfect, Bith!" was all the humbled squire could manage.

Endril grumbled that he thought it a waste of magic powers to use them in such a frivolous way, but Bith could see that he too was proud of her accomplishment and the pleasure it brought Cal. The young squire held the cloth close to him as if to verify it was real.

"How did you do that?" he started to ask, but Endril waved him off.

"Never ask a magician how he or she performed such and such a feat, or the illusion might be shattered," he warned, but the flag was not chimera, it was a solid piece of ancient felt with all the proper markings. With great care Cal rolled it up again, but instead of stuffing it back into his carry-sack, he tucked it gently inside his tunic.

The next morning the marchers reported less painful feet, but whether Cal's trick had worked for them or they were simply getting used to blisters and bunions, he did not know. The snow in the deepest part of the forest was less troublesome, not because it was any less thick, but because in the two weeks since Hathor had been carted across it, the snow had frozen more solidly. As they traveled farther from the salty dampness of the coast and closer to the chill mountain air, the temperature dropped rapidly.

As they tramped along, the villagers struck up a sea chantey to step to. While aboard the boats after their escape they had never sung, perhaps because of their mood of defeat and dejection. Cal, Bith, and Endril listened appreciatively as Valdspar, sailor-turned-soldier, rang the verses in a loud voice, then the whole file joined in on the choruses:

VERSE: Many a man has put to sea
To find himself fish, fame or fortune
And many a man has come to me
The maiden on the bottom.

CHORUS: Wail, wail, the wild wind blows down
Up, up, the sea stands tall
Hail, hail, the snows do roar round
Down, down, the boats do fall!

VERSE: I take the loser and the winner
And the good with the bad I take often

It makes no difference be you saint or sinner
To the maiden on the bottom.

CHORUS: Wail, wail, etc.

VERSE: So bow your head and say your prayers
Winter spring summer and autumn
Be humble and don't put on airs
Or you'll meet the maiden on the bottom.

CHORUS: Wail, wail, etc.

Endril, who always appreciated a good melody, clapped
his hands in delight and sang along with the chorusers after
the second verse. The ballad was not endless as Endril's
name-poem was, but there were scores of verses, each one
ending with the rollicking chorus lines. The music took the
men's minds off their feet and lifted their spirits. The arduous miles passed unnoticed, and by the end of the day they
had made fair progress toward the looming cliff face that
marked entry into the dominion of the legendary queen.

"Tomorrow we'll find out if she's real or not," Cal
declared with obvious satisfaction. Battling ghosts was
Bith's specialty, not his. For him the prospect of direct
confrontation was like a whetting of his appetite. Endril
had searched out a hidden gully just off the main trail where
they could camp without attracting undue attention, though
it was difficult to conceal such a large party of men. This
night he suggested to Cal that no fires be lit for security's
sake, but Cal felt that it was more important for his troop
to have a warm blaze and a hot meal.

"A man shouldn't have to fight with cold porridge in
his belly," was his soldierly answer. The gully was a frozen
streambed with sloping sides. Cal posted guards at each end
of the narrow camp, with a double guard at the upstream end
where in spring the melting snow from the mountains would

rush down to fill and overflow this path. Wood was gathered and soon a decent fire sprang up. Cal instructed his men to dry their flag strips so that in the morning they could wrap them freshly warm around their boots. As before, the three wanderers drew off to one side a little to converse among themselves, allowing the villagers to feel more comfortable in their own group, as was natural, for as Cal had explained, soldiers lose respect for their officers if they try to be too friendly with them. A man wants a leader he can respect.

"We always seem to be attacking the high ground from below," Endril commented dryly. "Why do you suppose that is?"

"Because we're not fat lords and ladies locked up safe in our castles and halls," Cal answered with a sneer.

"Careful there, Cal. We have royalty in our midst."

"Not all lords and ladies are like Lord Threnod," Bith protested. "Some are kind and generous."

"If a ruler will share the profits and see that all are cared for, and the people work for him willingly, I won't begrudge him his larger house or his greater number of oxen and sheep. But a man should have a choice, and that's what Threnod took away from those folk," said Cal with a nod toward the villagers at the fire.

"Agreed," said Endril.

"I wish Hathor could be with us tomorrow. You don't suppose we'll find him here, then?" she asked again. Endril repeated his assertion that Hathor was almost certainly in the hands of the Wind-Websters, but that by taking on his captors one at a time, first this alleged queen, then the masters of Dripping Hall, they stood a better chance of winning.

"We'd stand a better chance of winning if Hathor was at our side," Bith repeated, but there was nothing to be done for it.

"Have you not another brilliant battle plan, then, Bith?"

"I have not."

"Perhaps there won't be a battle. Perhaps we'll find an empty nest in that eagle's eyrie," Endril suggested.

"Yes, and perhaps the earth really does ride upon the back of a turtle, as the ancients said," Cal jested.

"Perhaps." Endril was cool to Cal's friendly jibes. "Over hundreds of years I have learned not to guess about the future. What comes, comes. Even the greatest seers and prophets are wrong most of the time."

"What do you mean?" Cal asked hotly, for he felt that the elf was somehow making fun of him, as he usually was when his words were so maddeningly enigmatic.

"Only that tomorrow we may fight, or we may run, or we may stroll to the top of the mountain as if we were on a spring day's pleasant hike. We'll just have to wait to find out."

"Sometimes I see the future as plain as the lines on my hand," Bith, who had been silent during this exchange, said softly, wistfully, as if it were no great joy to have such visions. Cal and Endril looked at her curiously, but neither could think of anything to say to her, and she did not elaborate. Finally Cal stretched and yawned.

"Let's to bed early," Cal advised. "Tomorrow we scale the cliffs."

CHAPTER
12

Ripping at the mink's skin with his teeth, Hathor stripped hide from flesh with one ferocious twist of his powerful neck.

"Very good, troll. We want the furs for our lovely ladies' outer garments. We want them intact, and free of bloodstains. We want them clean and whole. You are the very best we've ever had at this job, do you know?" The royal purser was pleased with his handiwork. The acquisition of this troll had turned out to be one of the best buys of his career. The thing was a slaughtering machine, and tireless.

For Hathor, this work was even more demeaning than his usual duties as butcher, for in the fur room the flesh went uneaten, wasted, left to rot or thrown to the dogs. This was near sacrilege to Hathor, who lived close to the earth, indeed sometimes within the earth, and had come to respect all living things. This was gross disrespect, to raise animals for their furs without even using their meat when you slew them. But he unquestioningly carried out every duty set before him, for his spirit was well nigh broken. No thankless chore was too hideous, no brutal assignment too degrading for the unswerving steadiness of the troll. His axe rose and fell, the blood spurted. And on and on he went. His keepers tested him repeatedly, as when they sent him to skin furs from minks, but nothing seemed to penetrate the troll's thick skin. He had stopped crying days ago, because he had no more tears. He continued to lose weight as his miserable diet barely provided him the minimum food for survival. His gaolers thought that he would slip back to his meat-eating ways if surrounded by all that temptation. Indeed, that was the Queen of Ice's whole plan for him—but it was not working. Instead of being enticed, Hathor was repulsed. The carnage, the waste, the sickeningly warm sticky smell of blood constantly in his nostrils, all combined to make him revile the very idea of eating flesh.

Despite Hathor's resistance, all this killing was taking its toll on his spirit. His eyes lost their luster and his face became set in a single expression of horror and exhaustion, so that even his fellow butchers began to avoid him. Then one day a load of hume corpses arrived, victims of some minor skirmish along the Wind-Websters' western border. (They were not the bodies of Websters—they themselves did not fight, preferring to hire mercenaries to do battle for them, just as they were hirelings of the Queen of Ice and saw nothing wrong or unusual in that arrangement.)

Hathor was sent to the charnel house, to perform the job of stripping the dead of their gold teeth. When he entered the holding room where the bodies lay, Hathor immediately recognized the signs of warfare, the stab wounds and the axe cuts, the limbs chopped by swords and faces smashed by maces. He registered a mild protest to the guard who accompanied him.

"They died fighting. Do they get honor?" Hathor asked awkwardly, for he was still uncomfortable with the language of humes, and these Wind-Websters spoke with a harsh, guttural accent that he sometimes did not understand. The guard laughed in his face.

"Sure, beast, they get honor. You can pull their teeth first!" With that Hathor was given a basket and a set of crude tongs and locked in with the corpses. This was the final shame, the last disgrace. Hathor sat down suddenly. A mist of blackness crept into his eyes. The ghosts of the fallen warriors rose up before him, screaming as if their wounds were freshly made. The heat and smoke of battle surrounded him. The moans of the dying assailed his ears. Hathor put his clumsy hands over his oversize ears and tried to block out the tortured cries, but still they came on. Then the animals started up, all those pigs and geese and chickens, the sheep and the mild-eyed oxen, loudly calling Hathor's name in their various tongues, accusing him, condemning him. Hathor scrambled to his feet and backed to the door as the corpses rose from their slabs and stepped toward him, the animals at their feet.

Troll madness is a terrible thing to behold. Hathor's eyes bulged, his tongue blackened and protruded, his face turned purple, and his neck muscles distended. With a roar that released the pent-up fury of two weeks of humiliation, Hathor put his fists through the wood beams of the charnel-house door and burst out, running over the guard without even noticing him. Starved, exhausted, and now insane, the demented troll flung himself blindly down a hallway, through a door, and into the weak northern sunlight. He looked around but saw nothing, for it was as if all the blood he had spilled was pouring over his eyes. He ran, not knowing where he went, knocking over soldiers and citizens haphazardly.

Twice round Dripping Hall he charged, strewing carts and stalls in his path, crushing phalanxes of soldiers who knew he was coming but still could not stop him. Finally they opened the front gate and steered him out on his third go-round, barricading all other ways with overturned wagons and herding him like a blind bull out the portal, but it made no difference to the crazed Hathor, who continued to bolt aimlessly to and fro just outside the tower until the palace guard set fierce black dogs on him, chasing him toward the far hills.

The royal purser was furious. His prized possession had escaped. He ordered a search begun as soon as he heard about the episode, but Hathor had disappeared. Within a day or two life in the tower city returned to its unruffled orderly ways, and the amusing but unfortunate "Weeping Butcher of Dripping Hall" was all but forgotten.

After he outran the dogs, for madness heightened his already prodigious strength, Hathor fell into a streambed. He lapped at the water like a dog himself, then rolled in the mud at the stream's edge until he had covered himself with dirt and twigs. Truly fearful-looking, he caught a glimpse of himself in a pool of water as he crawled away from the stream on all fours, but he did not recognize the grotesque filthy beast in the cloudy image.

"Stay away!" he shouted at his own reflection. "I kill everything. I steal from the dead." Then he was off and running again, sightless, crashing across the woodless plain. The whirring blades of the Wind-Websters' wind-looms in the distance were thrashing monsters—he ran away from them, at first toward the glowing barrier of the Mistwall, then, well before reaching the high dense barrier, veering away. At last, his skin lacerated by cuts and welts, his lungs burning and his eyes red orbs, Hathor fell in the open plain, miles from Dripping Hall.

Here it ends, Hathor thought, for he felt too weak to rise, and life began to seep from him like a fluid. The madness left him and was replaced by a sweet insouciance, a warm listlessness that crept into his limbs, rendering him helpless. He would die here uncomplainingly. Kestrals and corbies would pick his bones clean, and that would be the end of Hathor the troll.

As he lay on the ground, dirt-covered and bleeding, suddenly a soft feminine voice of infinite kindness whispered in his ears.

"Come, poor one. I can help you." Hathor opened one

reddened eye. Before him was a tiny creature, hume in shape but each feature in miniature, pale like the Wind-Websters but without their haughty features. She was dressed in a dainty smock, and she was quite old, Hathor could tell, though his bewildered brain could not make out much more than that. "Come," she repeated. Hathor struggled to his feet, holding a hand over his face that he knew to be ghastly.

"Who are you?" he managed to ask, but his rescuer only said "hush" and led him by the hand into a smallish, half-hidden dell where a copse of low ash trees surrounded a tiny thatched cabin, the only trees and the only house for miles around, tucked away in this one dip in the otherwise feature-less vastness of the plain. Far in the distance Hathor could still see the relentlessly circling scythes of the wind-looms, and overshadowing them the larger tower of Dripping Hall, but they were far away, their outlines softened and blurred in a haze of dust thrown up by farmers' plows and caught in the late-afternoon sun. Hathor was so tired. Never had he known such weariness. His little hostess brought him inside the cottage, but the single bed therein was much too small for his broad form, so she piled a bed of straw against the empty hearth and covered him with stuffed sewn bedding, and Hathor was soon taken into the healing arms of sleep.

CHAPTER
13

The villagers of Steadfast-by-Sea proved skillful mountain climbers, applying their sea skills with ropes and their agility clambering up masts to good effect, scaling the rocky promontories with ease and hauling up their supplies after them. Cal had decided to avoid the single path that led to the mountaintop retreat, attempting instead a difficult ascent up the north face of the mountain. By doing this he hoped to retain some element of surprise, though he was uncertain just what he would find at the summit. Even with the agile seamen leading the way, however, the going was rough. Several times the whole party had to back down from impassable cul-de-sacs in search of another route to the top. Twice Bith had to be carried upward on the shoulders of another climber, for her delicate hands were unsuited to gripping the icy rock, and once she was ported up to a cliff face in a sling like so much baggage. But all in all the group struggled valiantly, and by late afternoon they all clung precariously to a narrow ledge just beneath the surprisingly broad campground beneath the final lair of the Queen of Ice. The sounds and smells of a lively encampment carried over the rim to them. The travel-weary villagers dreamt ruefully of their faraway wives and children, but Cal traversed the narrow ledge, passing from man to man, checking on each soldier's condition, and complimenting them on their superior climbing abilities, and slowly the mood of the group improved.

"Just two tasks remain before us, then you can build boats and ride the mountain's fast-flowing rivers toward home," he told them. "First we must fight this queen, if she exists, then we must free our friend. After that, we release you from your obligations." Cal had told them of the original purpose of the mission, to investigate the purported rip in the Mistwall, but these isolated villagers lived far from the threatening curtain of mist. Their lives had never been affected by its encroachment, but as a former foot soldier Cal knew that men fight better when they know what it is they're fighting for. He did not ask them to join this quest, nor did he expect them to volunteer. If they could help deliver Hathor from his captors, that would be enough.

The wind tried to push them off the cliff, but they held on, waiting steadfastly as befitted their place-name. Cal had ordered a night attack. He hoped to rout the camp followers and avoid a confrontation on the open ground, then attack the upper castle his advance scouts had observed. In many ways his strategy resembled the victorious battle at Steadfast-by-Sea, without Bith's incendiary performance. But this time his plans went all awry.

The queen disdained even to make an appearance. As the last campfires dimmed to glowing ashes, the raiding party crept stealthily over the rim. But as soon as they appeared, black-garbed soldiers began pouring out of the gate at the foot of the peak. It was a trap! There was no one in the camp—the populace had been evacuated within the mountain. Instead of a disorganized, sleep-slowed camp, the outnumbered invaders faced a charging mass of well-armed troops. The tiny force had nowhere to go; climbing up the cliff face had been difficult enough. It would be suicide to attempt a descent.

Endril and Bith had held back as part of the plan, to allow Cal and his men to launch an assault unimpeded, and to give Endril firing range for the deadly darts from his bow. By the time Cal realized what he had stumbled into, he and his men were well into the center of the deserted camp. They were soon cut off from Endril and Bith by an encircling movement of the queen's guard. Rallying the terror-stricken villagers around him, Cal formed a crude phalanx and attempted to push toward the trail-head that led down the mountain, but the leader of the queen's troops sensed his movement and cut off his escape route by sending a detachment larger than Cal's entire group to blockade it. Off to one side Cal glimpsed Valdspar take a wicked sword cut across his side. He fell among the fighting mob, and Cal did not see him rise.

Slowly Cal and his men were backed up toward the cliff edge. Peering over at the riotous scene, Bith cursed, then shouted at Endril above the battle's din: "We made a mistake!"

"No fooling!" Endril answered succinctly between steady shots from his twanging bow.

"The spirit messenger from the Claviger told us only Hathor could defeat our enemy, but we forgot, and attacked anyway."

"We don't have Hathor," was Endril's tart reply.

"But suppose we could make them think we did, even for a few moments?" said Bith with a strange smile.

"Yes, do it!" The quick-witted elf grasped her idea at once. There was no time to tell Cal, who was fighting for his life only a few feet away from them. Bith huddled behind Endril. From one of her many pockets she pulled a thick stubby candle, a flint and stone, and some dried sawdust shavings. The high, cold wind threatened to scatter the tiny pile she made of the wood slivers, but she patiently coaxed a little fire to life, and working quickly, she burnt her delicate fingers while fashioning an image of the lost troll from the pliant wax. When she was satisfied with the likeness, she sprinkled salt on the fire, then water, all the while holding the doll figure in one hand while chanting in a low voice:

"In this image life to be
The everlasting mystery
Rise, O spirit, from the flame
He and not he—Hathor by name!"

At first nothing happened. The bloody battle in the camp continued. Two more of the villagers fell to the slashing halberds of the queen's men, and the attackers pressed their advantage, ruthlessly driving the villagers toward the cliff edge and death. Just as the contest reached its most desperate stage, Hathor appeared suddenly in the midst of the enemy, several times his normal size, a giant troll with axe upraised and a savage expression on his face. Chaos in the enemy's ranks ensued. The oversize Hathor neither moved nor spoke, but his appearance was enough to scatter soldiers left and right.

"Quickly, while they are distracted," Endril called to Cal. A group of soldiers still blocked the main path down, but Cal luckily discovered the smaller trail out to the west, toward the land of the Wind-Websters. The remaining sea fighters followed their crestfallen leader in a pell-mell retreat, Bith and Endril scampering along behind. The conjured image was already fading with a curious afterglow, but the illusory Hathor had done his job. The foiled attempt at seizing the queen's icy fortress was neither a victory nor a defeat, but it had been costly. When they reassembled in the western foothills, only seventeen of the original twenty villagers remained. After they had put some distance between themselves and their pursuers, they stopped to dress each other's wounds and mourn their lost companions. Bith explained to Cal as much as she could of what she had done.

"That was not Hathor," said Cal emphatically. The sight

had startled him, but he knew that it was Bith's handiwork almost from the start.

"No, it was—how shall I describe it?—his spirit form summoned. But did you notice how thin he was?"

"I noticed how *big* he was."

"No, that part was my doing, but his face was so bony, I fear he is not being treated well."

"If that is so, they will pay," Cal swore.

"Enough," said Endril, who was tenderly swabbing a seaman's scraped leg with some strange ointment. "We may not have conquered the Queen of Ice—"

"We did not even see her—" Cal broke in.

"But we cut a week off the journey by taking the mountain route."

"At great cost," said Cal somberly, for he grieved greatly over the three lost villagers, whose bodies had been left on the field of battle. His troops were a dispirited lot. Valdspar had indeed been among the fallen, and though Sheerstrake had made the black guard pay in blood, now he wandered the camp like an unhappy ghost in search of his brother who would never return. Many of the others had suffered wounds and scrapes that would have become infected and possibly gangrenous without Endril's healing balms. Only the great distance they had covered (and the formidable barrier of the mountain they had trekked and fought their way over) prevented them from turning toward home at once. They clung to Cal's promise of a quick boat trip downriver as their best hope of ever again seeing their homeland and families.

Now the three adventurers and their ragged band were faced with another decision. As soon as they left the leafy cover of the forested foothills, they would be traveling in open plain country again as they entered the land of the Wind-Websters.

"Bith's ruse may have made the queen suspect that Hathor has escaped. Or if she's smart, she'll know it was magic by her troops' description of the scene. Either way, though, she's likely to show up at Dripping Hall if she even suspects we're heading that way."

"We still don't know for sure if she even exists," said Cal.

"Whose castle do you think those soldiers were guarding?" Endril asked with a wry look about him. "She's real, alright. And only Hathor can defeat her, for whatever reasons. So the sooner we find him the better off we are. We need to have some means of entering the Hall when we get there, without attacking."

"To pose as someone you are not is dangerous for a soldier. Spies are usually hung," Cal objected.

"We've tried a direct assault twice now. This time we have to be more subtle, my young friend."

"What if we pose as slave traders ourselves? These Wind-Websters seem to be great ones for having others do their work for them. What if the three of us were to bring them a shipment of hardy seafolk to work their waterways?"

"Would your bunch submit to that?" Endril asked Cal in a low voice.

"I think so, but I'll have to ask them. This is not something a military leader can order someone to do. It calls for volunteers." With that Cal rose from the log where he was resting and marched stiffly to the circle of villagers, who as usual had gathered off to one side from the three. Bith noticed for the first time that Cal was favoring his left leg, and she saw dried blood on the back of his breeches.

"You ought to tend to him next," she told Endril, who had finished caring for the villagers' injuries.

"He wouldn't let me. I think he wants to feel the pain of defeat," said Endril. They both watched as Cal spoke quietly with the somber men. He returned with a grim expression of fierce determination thrusting his jaw forward.

"They all volunteered, even Sheerstrake, who only hours ago lost his kinsman Valdspar," he told Bith and Endril through clenched teeth. "Wonderful men. This time I mustn't let them down. They say they will fight for the sake of their fallen companions."

"Excellent. This is one time we can be thankful we don't have our beloved troll with us," Endril noted. "There's no disguising him. But if I dye my beard and Bith cuts her hair—"

"Again?" Bith cried.

"And Cal exchanges his chain mail and weapons of war for tradesman's garb, we might pass for a party of merchants come to barter slaves for goods."

"It's a risky plan, but I see no alternative," said Cal.

"Then we are agreed. We ought to make our preparations now, for as soon as we broach the plain we'll be visible to all," Endril warned.

"We really should have a wagon for transporting our 'slaves,'" Cal pointed out.

"It may be that we can trade for one on the main road into Dripping Hall. Until then, we'll rope them together. Of course they'll have to disarm also."

Soon an amazing transformation had taken place among the group. The seamen played their part, ripping their clothes and generally disheveling themselves, though it was hard for them to remove the look of newly freed men from their eyes. Having suffered bondage under Lord Threnod, they knew how terrible a thing it was to men's spirits, so when it came time to accept being lashed together with hempen leads there were a few grumbles, but in the main they submitted to the ruse with dignity.

Bith emerged from behind a bush looking more like a young gentleman than Cal ever had. She had cropped her hair close and pulled a cap down over the remaining bit so that she looked boyish, and with a borrowed pair of Cal's breeches and a tucked-in shirt she passed for the very image of a tradesman's apprentice. Endril aged before their eyes, assuming the patrician's look with his wispy beard a distinguished grey and his hair likewise. Cal did what he could to hide his soldierly manner, but it was difficult for him to imagine himself as a mere dealer of goods, and a slave trader at that. He gave up his chain mail and sword but refused to part with his boots, and thus was forced to hide them beneath the skirts of a foppishly long robe. All in all they passed for a less-than-prosperous caravan of traders with a small string of slaves, but robust, healthy ones, a good prize for some wealthy landowner among the Wind-Websters.

In the new scheme of things, Endril and Bith took the lead in their roles as chief trader and his "boy," followed by the line of bondsmen, with Cal bringing up the rear as guard. Soon they were all gazing in wonderment at the sight of the fabled wind-looms. The road to Dripping Hall was dusty, illustrating how dry the land would be without the ceaseless working of the looms. Water pumped by the looms trickled down furrows stretched in neat rows along either side of the road. This ingenious and clever irrigation system was the second great innovation of the Wind-Websters, after the looms. Near the river, where the land was too saturated by water, the wind-looms were turned to another use, drawing the water from the ground and draining it away by means of siphons connected to pipes and tunnels. Thus the wind-looms functioned both to bring water to dry land and take it away from wetlands.

"Truly they are great engineers. If only they didn't depend on slave labor to run them, these would be marvels indeed, and the Wind-Websters a great people," was Endril's commentary.

"Like these towers, they are too proud and arrogant," said Cal. "They are too impressed by their own achievements. This makes them treat others with disdain."

"Except the Queen of Ice," said Bith.

"Except the queen," Cal agreed, "with whom they have made a strange alliance. It's a wonder they don't destroy each other, these partners in evil."

"Given time, they would," Endril said emphatically, with that world-weary voice that implied vast knowledge of things past. Endril knew that arrogant people always have cause to repent, and that justice might work slowly but it always works, bringing down the high and exalting the low. These and many other things he knew, the peculiar elf whose name was a fragment of endless ethereal music.

"Hush now, and play your parts. Here comes another convoy up behind us," Bith warned. They pulled the villagers aside to let a long rumbling formation of carts pass them. In the carts were dozens of dark-skinned, vicious-looking orcs, fighting among each other and rattling the wooden staves of the cart, a violent bunch still untamed after days and days in captivity. Endril ventured a comment to one of the passing traders, walking alongside the man's wagon to converse.

"The Wind-Websters' whips will flog the spirit out of them," the trader spat in reply. He was a fat hume, greasy and greedy-looking, who took poor care of his captives and eyed Endril's getup and his string of slaves with suspicion.

"You needn't fatten them up for market," he told Endril sarcastically. "These buyers want oxen, not well-fed hogs."

Endril made some excuse about their being fresh meat, not yet seasoned, and the trader acknowledged the possibility.

"A new raid, eh? Where did you cull them from? I thought this territory was pretty well hunted out."

"That's my secret," Endril said shortly, and he dropped off from the fast walking pace he'd been keeping. The surprised trader looked back at Endril with hate and increased suspicion.

"That was foolish. I'm afraid I've made an enemy," Endril scolded himself, but the others seemed to think it added to their credibility as traders.

"He didn't even look at me," Bith marveled, for as a beautiful if somewhat gawky young woman she was beginning to receive admiring glances from men wherever she went.

"May it remain so," said Cal, for he too had begun to

notice those looks, and where Bith saw admiration, he saw lechery and lust. Cal believed that a true knight was courteous to women, and respectful.

"We didn't look cruel or rapacious enough, that was the problem," Endril stated. "It's difficult for an actor to put enough brutishness in his or her face to be convincing."

"I'll try," Cal said with a swagger, and he ran back to pretend to castigate the villagers for the benefit of the last of the passing train of wagons.

"Alright you beasts, up now. You've had enough rest! Eat the dust from the wagon wheels, for that'll be your dinner."

From within their cages the orcs looked hungrily at the rugged villagers, whom they would have killed and devoured given the chance. The thought of being put in with those subhuman creatures put fear in the hearts of the villagers, much more than Cal's halfhearted harangue. So far the men had uncomplainingly done everything Cal had asked of them, but he could not expect them to walk unarmed into cages full of orcs. The ruse must end as soon as they were within the palace walls, certainly before any auction took place. This pretended cruelty was as hard on him as it was on them, for he loved them so for their valor and loyalty to him. This was his first, albeit limited, command, and he had enjoyed it until he had tasted defeat at the palace of the Queen of Ice. Now it tore at Cal's heart to have to affect heartlessness to these same warriors. But as they trudged closer to Dripping Hall, he was forced to act out this deception more and more as they were repeatedly passed by other groups of traders and merchants. Before long he regretted agreeing to the idea, as a group of soldiers bullied their way past him and he could only smile and bow as befitted a defenseless peddler of goods.

"If another one of those mercenary thugs shoves me, there's going to be blood on the road," Cal whispered to Endril.

"Calm yourself, Cal. We are too close now to drop our disguises."

"Very well, but I make no assurances once we attain the palace. I won't see these brave fellows caged with orcs and trolls, Hathor or no Hathor."

"Nor shall you have to," Endril promised him.

Like Hathor, they arrived on a busy market day. It seemed that the whole population of the countryside was trying to crowd into the single main gate through the sloping tower of Dripping Hall. The bladeless cone of the castle projected stolidity and stability, surrounded by the smaller whirring looms of its active neighbors. Today it was especially merry-looking. The exterior of the Hall had been festooned with twisted colored paper strings and draped with flags and pennants encircling its rounded peak like pendants. A local festival was in full swing when the band of three and seventeen took their place in line to enter the palace. The gala spilled out of the circular inner area (where Hathor had careened about before escaping) onto the flat ground outside the Hall where others waited to gain entrance. Pie-sellers jostled with penny-bakers and candy-men as the eager crowd began trading, buying, and bartering even before reaching the market.

"How much for the whole lot?" a semidrunken merchant accosted Endril, tugging at his ill-fitting costume with a shaky hand.

"I'll get a better price inside," Endril responded.

"Aye," the merchant replied with a sly look, "but out here you don't have to pay the Dripping Hall tax."

"I'll pay," Endril snapped. This was apparently the right answer, for the merchant suddenly dropped his insistence and walked away.

"That was no besotted merchant but an agent of the Hall, I'll wager."

"Who rules Dripping Hall, anyway?" Cal asked as they waited in line.

"A Council, nominally. The Wind-Websters don't trust

any one of their own to take power. But if you ask me they're under the thumb of the queen now. They've chosen the wrong ally—she's too powerful for them."

"As to that, I care not a whit. Let them slaughter each other, just don't let them threaten my countrymen nor my country."

"If we succeed, you won't have to worry about that. If we fail . . ." Endril let the unfinished thought fade into silence. The chill north wind cut at them where they stood. Far away at the edge of the horizon the Mistwall pulsated unevenly, a thin band at the line where earth met sky, unnatural, almost alive. The distant cloud bothered Bith most of all, though she would not admit it. Hers were the most vivid and terrifying memories of what the Mistwall could do to a person, a city, a country. To take her mind off the remembered horrors, Bith pranced up and down the line, playing the adolescent boy to the hilt, affecting a manly swagger of her slim hips and playing harmless tricks as young boys are wont to do. Cal thought it dangerous to draw attention to themselves, but Endril assured him that she knew what she was doing. Bith pulled the tail of a trader's donkey and had to dodge a swift hind-leg kick by somersaulting backward. Then from somewhere she produced three stuffed rag balls and began juggling them deftly.

"Where did she learn to do that? I wonder," said Cal.

"Those who know magic and the jongleurs are not so far apart," Endril told him as they watched together from their place in line. "And in the palace where she grew up there must have been many entertainers to amuse the children of royalty."

After a couple of cartwheels and some chasing after a loose fowl, Bith returned to the group, breathless but exhilarated.

"How did I do?" she asked Endril, and Cal realized that once again they had been scheming without informing him.

"Excellent, my dear. Charming performance." Naturally one couldn't tell whether or not Endril was being sarcastic.

"Will it suffice?"

"I think so."

"What is all this about?" Cal asked, but at that moment the crowd shuffled forward and they were jostled from behind. Two of their men were knocked to the ground, and Cal rushed back to see them up, though he was careful not to show pity, but instead yelled at them for their clumsiness. They were almost at the gate when another commotion broke out ahead. There were shouts and curses and a sudden yell of pain, and the line was disrupted. Cal reached automatically for his sword and did not find it. Just then a man burst out of the gate, pursued by a dozen soldiers. He ran right by Cal, who happened to be standing out from the file by a few feet. Even in the excitement of the moment, Cal sized up the situation with a cool head—that was what made him a good soldier. The man was an escaped slave. Instead of tripping him up, as he might have done easily, Cal quickly faked a bumbling ineptness and stumbled in the soldiers' path, knocking off the two lead pursuers and giving the runner at least a chance of reaching freedom. But on the open plain, with the whole crowd waiting to enter Dripping Hall roaring and cheering, he was quickly hunted down and dragged back "to be fed to the orcs" as they heard one man surmise.

One of the returning soldiers singled out Cal. "Stupid weakling. Why didn't you help us? Instead you got in the way, you worthless money-grubber." Cal grit his teeth but smiled and said nothing. Just before they would have entered, they found their way blocked by a double row of soldiers who burst from the gate to push the crowd back on both sides.

"The queen arrives," Endril guessed, and almost as soon as he spoke black-caped advance riders appeared at the horizon in the distance, pounding down the road to Dripping Hall. Behind the distant drumming of the horses' hooves came the royal cortege, a black and gold wagon of immense size, so huge that even from afar it was clear that the vehicle could never pass through the relatively narrow portal of the palace.

"How did they get that monster down the mountain?" Cal wondered.

"Better yet, how do they get it back up?" Bith added. Endril solved the mystery in curt words.

"They don't," he said in a low voice. "That ostentatious carriage is for use on these plains only. I suppose she was carried down by litter. Cal, get back," he warned. "You're the only one they got a good look at in the fight. The villagers' injuries make them more convincing as slaves than we are as masters. It looks as though we've beaten them."

A haughty Wind-Webster, one of the purser's functionaries, stood at the gate and announced: "There'll be no more entries to Dripping Hall today. Come back tomorrow."

"Apparently it's a surprise visit, no doubt engendered by Bith's little ghost-of-Hathor trick," Endril spoke in satisfied tones. "Now all the elements are in place for a final battle."

"Except the real Hathor, we haven't got him," said Bith.

"Oh, he's here, make no mistake. We've only to find him."

"How are we to do that if we can't even get inside the castle?" Cal asked impatiently as the crowd milled around them.

"We come back tomorrow, as the official said," Endril answered dryly. "But for now let's see if we can catch a glimpse of her as she makes her regal entrance." They moved off to one side, prodded by the halberds of the palace guard. Many of the outlander traders were setting up camp as close to the gate as the Wind-Websters' mercenaries would let them, to keep their place in line. Multicolored tents of many shapes and sizes were blooming like giant flowers all around them, and a brisk trade sprang up almost before the gate of Dripping Hall swung shut.

It turned out that there would be no sighting of the Queen

of Ice this day. Her plains-wagon was so huge it doubled as living quarters. Most of her horsemen arrived ahead of her and drew up in a circle open at one end, which quickly closed up as soon as the carriage entered it. Thus surrounded, the movable throne was secured from immediate threat, though a large force could certainly overwhelm it.

"Why doesn't she enter the Hall?" Bith asked.

"She is not their sovereign," Endril explained, "though she might as well be, for she controls them as surely as these wind-looms draw water. Perhaps she finds her own compartment more comfortable. These Wind-Websters have much ingenuity and engineering but lack a sense of enjoyment of life."

"I suspect it's a matter of security," Cal countered. "She feels most secure within her ring of riders."

"True enough."

"Look!" Bith said suddenly. She pointed beyond Dripping Hall to the south. The far-off Mistwall was flaring and rising. The split in its uniform denseness was growing, and one could see the cold wind rushing through it, sucked to the other side by the rapid change in pressure. On this side of the Mistwall a thunderhead formed a fast-moving storm that detached itself and careened over the open plain, sending down funnels of swirling wind. Though it was many miles from Dripping Hall and the impromptu encampment of the traders outside its shoring, the storm stirred the wind even here, sending the blades of neighboring wind-looms into a spinning frenzy, tugging at the newly pegged tents, ripping at flaps and pennants. The festive decorations atop Dripping Hall were torn from where they hung and sent flying over the landscape.

"We ought to make some preparations for the night ourselves," Cal suggested, for as the spontaneous village had formed they had become somewhat conspicuous as they stood uncertainly amid the activity of others making camp.

"With what?" Bith asked sulkily. "We have no tents."

"Perhaps we can trade for some cover. What do we have to offer?" Endril inquired, but the three of them were warriors now, they traveled light, and Bith could produce a few worthless baubles as barter.

"We could trade away one of our 'slaves,'" Endril offered. Cal was shocked and offended, but Bith furthered the idea.

"Yes, if we could find someone who would take delivery tomorrow," Bith joked, but that gave Endril an idea.

"Indeed, we could sell the whole lot today and be done with it."

"Another deceit?" Cal scoffed, for he was tired of these deceptions and longed only for a personal confrontation with the queen and her horsemen.

"Yes, Cal, unless you want to shiver in the open tonight."

"I've done so before," he responded, but by that time Endril had already strolled off to mingle with assorted buyers, sellers, and swappers. In a few minutes he returned.

"Come," he said. "I've met an acquaintance. We shan't have to sell our slaves nor suffer outside. His tent has room for us all."

"Who is it?" Bith asked.

"A distant relation."

"Another elf?" Cal asked in surprise, for to his knowledge elves never acted as traders, despising the materialism of enterprise.

"No, a court musician. His fellow merrymakers have been delayed and his tent is fortuitously half-empty. Come."

Darkness was sweeping across the plain, hastened by the storm blowing up from the tear in the Mistwall, as the three fatigued adventurers and their weary string of villager "slaves" entered the tent of Endril's cousin many-times-removed.

"Tomorrow we find Hathor and fight!" Cal said determinedly as he looked around in the dimness. There was but a single personage inside the tent, an elf proportioned more typically than Endril, that is, smaller.

Endril began to make introductions: "This is my twenty-sixth cousin, Randil. Sing us your name, cuz." The diminutive elf responded with a snippet of lovely a cappella. Endril answered with his own name in music, and soon the two were trading melodies and had completely forgotten the others. Cal and Bith waited for a while, then gave up on being formally introduced and made ready for sleep. They removed the ropes around the villagers' ankles so they could rub their sore skin. Cal treated them personally with salve he'd commandeered from Endril earlier.

The tent was nearly bare because the other music-makers in Randil's party carried most of the provisions and equipment, so all had to make do with what they themselves carried. They were lulled to sleep tht night by the endless round of gentle singing that Bith and Cal knew was merely an extended introduction between two elves whose names were eternally everlastingly intertwined.

CHAPTER
14

Not far away, inside the hut nestled amid the ash grove in the little hidden dell, Hathor awoke to the most delicious aromas he had ever smelt. It seemed to him that all his life he had waited for such wonderful scents to summon him. His hunger was ferocious. At the oven of the cottage was his rescuer, the tiny woman who had found him, half-dead, and brought him to this secluded sanctuary. He rose eagerly, then lay back and groaned in pain as his sore muscles protested the deed.

The woman at her stove spoke to him without turning around: "There's a place of hot stones in the back. Go sit there for a while, then come in and we'll break your fast."

A place of hot stones, Hathor repeated to himself, wondering what that meant. In back of the cottage was a smaller wooden structure, not much larger than a winter vegetable larder. Inside there was indeed a pile of steaming stones heaped over the hot ashes of a peat fire. Hathor shut the door behind him and soon found that though the tiny room was hot, it was not completely uncomfortable. He lay on the single wooden bench in the room and began to sweat out the accumulated dirt of two weeks of captivity. It felt as if his whole body were purging itself of the horror of the past few days, the blood and the killing. When the heat became too extreme, he stepped outside. Seeing a patch of early snow under the ash trees, Hathor rolled in it and rubbed himself with the icy slush, then entered the heat room again and repeated the process, sweating until he could no longer tolerate the warmth of the stones, then giving himself an icy rubdown in the snow.

"The room is so hot, I had to jump in snow," Hathor announced as he reentered the cottage.

"Nonsense," the woman answered briskly, but in a sweet, kindly voice. "I used it myself this morning and I let it cool down before I put you in," she said with a smile. "And as to jumping in the snowdrift, that's exactly what you're supposed to do after. Come, sit, I will feed you."

Hathor drew up a place on a stool too small for him before a table too low for him. The woman withdrew a tray of steaming rolls and placed them on a plate in front of Hathor. She set a crock of butter and one of honey next to the still-hot bread. Before Hathor would eat, though, he asked her name.

"I am Kneadmora, your ally. You do not know it, but you were sent to me. Now, eat, while the bread is still soft and hot."

Hathor was used to dry crackers and crumbly low breads. Never had he eaten such savory, sweet, puffy concoctions as these. He finished a plateful without effort.

"Good. What is it?" Hathor asked in his usual simple way.

"It is bread," Kneadmora answered, equally straightforward.

"I have eaten bread before, but none like this."

"Then I will show you how to make it, after breakfast. Try some of these," she offered, filling his plate again with a new trayful of beautifully glazed pastries, fluffy and flaky, that needed no honey or butter to sweeten them.

"You say I was sent to you—" Hathor began between mouthfuls, but Kneadmora put him off with a tender pat on the head (she had to reach up though he was sitting and she standing).

"Not now, brave troll. First, you eat. Then we have a baking lesson. Then perhaps we talk about tomorrow."

"I fight tomorrow?" Hathor winced. Despite the soothing steam, his body was still bruised from two weeks of beatings and abuse.

"Eat. Bake. Then we see about tomorrow," Kneadmora repeated.

Hathor complied, stuffing himself with the mouth-watering baked goods Kneadmora supplied him by the panful. At last Hathor ate his fill, and half crawled back to the bedding for a nap, and for the first time in many a sleep instead of nightmares there came to him a pleasant dream of his one glorious night with the troll women of Ausviget. When he awoke there was yet another meal prepared and waiting for him at the child-size table. On a separate table where she worked, Kneadmora had laid out the utensils of her trade, the bowls and stirrers, the flour, butter, and sugar, the flat stone where even now she was pounding away at a pliant lump of dough.

"Eat again, my fine one. Then come here and take your lesson."

Curious as he was, Hathor could not resist the wafting fragrance of the hot bread that awaited him. A pitcher of goat's milk stood in a ceramic mug next to the plate of bread, already sliced and heaped with farmer's cheese. He finished the lot.

When Kneadmora was sure that he was satisfied, she led him by the hand, commenting as she did: "You have bak-er's hands. It is no good for the dough if your palms are sweaty—but yours are cool and dry. It must be that cave dwelling."

Hathor, who was self-conscious about his rough features now that he spent most of his time in the company of humans, was pleased to hear that his great paws were useful for something besides swinging an axe. He stood by patiently while Kneadmora showed him how to sift flour, the first step in making temsebread.

"What does sifting it do?" he asked.

"It's part of the magic," Kneadmora answered with a crinkly smile and a wink of her bright eyes. "Now we add the other ingredients, then knead it and let it sit, for you cannot rush such sacred preparations. But here I have some in a further stage. Now comes the kneading. Here, you try, you should be good at this," she ordered Hathor, and the obedient troll, who could have crushed the tiny old woman with one sweep of his mighty arm, allowed himself to be dressed in an apron and meekly took his place at the baker's table. "Slam the dough down on the table, don't be bashful. Again! Again! Now, fold it, massage it, knead, knead, knead. Good!"

Hathor found the activity soothing. As he worked the dough he could feel it almost coming alive in his hands. Later, when he saw how much it grew in the bowl while rising, he knew that there was indeed magic in Kneadmora's methods. Why had he been led into the care of this unusual person? He did not know. Then he realized with a wonderful rare sort of certainty that this was the person who could answer his question; he had but to ask.

"Why do I want to eat meat?" he asked bluntly. Kneadmora did not seem surprised by the question.

"Oh, that is easy. Is that all that troubles you? Well, your ancestors were meat-eaters, and you came from them. But more than mere habit, hume and troll alike foolishly believe that eating life will give life. It does not. The spirit in the flesh cannot be eaten. It is set free when the body dies. And plant-eaters may be as strong as meat-eaters. Is the wolf stronger than the ox that eats only hay? Besides, who says it is better to be strong? Some say gentleness is the greatest virtue, because human beings are not gentle by nature."

"Trolls not gentle either," Hathor said sadly. Then: "I

want to stay here. I want to learn all about this."

"After the morrow, if you are victorious, there will be plenty of time for lessons. And you will win."

"What must I do? I cannot fight the whole city."

"You are to challenge the queen to single combat, an old and honored tradition. Despite the fact that she is queen and a woman, she cannot refuse you. However, she can name a champion, and she will do so. That is who you must fight."

"Who is her champion?"

"Alas, I do not know."

This news troubled Hathor, for he knew he was not in fighting trim. A single day of recuperation would not heal two weeks' weakening of his battered body.

"I ache," he told Kneadmora as they worked together at the baking table.

"Come, lie down," she ordered him. The surprisingly spry old woman then knelt and began to knead Hathor's sore shoulders with strong, supple fingers, as if he were a giant lump of dough. She seemed to know exactly where to apply pressure, where her fingers could soothe a bruise here and massage a knot there, until his limbs began to relax and his stiff neck became flexible again. The treatment lasted a long time, until Hathor was drowsy.

"Now, to the hot stones again, then sleep. When you awake, your body will be renewed."

Kneadmora was right. In a single day, by means of the sweat baths and massage, and huge helpings of her magic bread, Hathor recovered to a remarkable degree the strength that was innately his. When he awoke the next morning, again to the sweet scents of baking bread, he stretched and yawned deeply. A twinge or two reminded him of his ordeal, but he felt refreshed and invigorated. Kneadmora had washed and patched his clothes.

"Why do you do all this for me?" he asked when they sat down together for the morning meal.

"It is not the evil only who have allies. Claviger and maybe your friend Vili sent me. They do not want the forces of the Queen of Ice to sweep out of the north and join forces with the Dark Lord. Good must win, as good always does in the end. Besides," she said with a delightful smile, "I have a personal interest in this battle. What would happen to bread-bakers like myself if the meat-eaters took over the world?" With that she rose and popped another loaf into the glowing oven, leaving Hathor to wonder at the fates of men and trolls and the ways of the gods.

CHAPTER
15

Kneadmora stood at the door to her hut and waved Hathor good-bye. In his new sack were the gifts she had given him: a fine screen of woven grass for sifting flour, a pan to bake it in, and, most precious of all, a book of recipes. Though Hathor could not read, this was a special book that pictured everything and illustrated the steps—indeed there were no words in the book, instead handsome drawings that he could follow easily. In the few hours she had spent with him, Kneadmora had imparted the essence of baking: treat the dough with love and respect and you can make it into anything. A changed troll, Hathor now knew that he no longer had to make do with root vegetables, those dirty turnips and the like. Now he could bake! Hathor hiked the short climb out of the hidden valley onto the broader expanse. Pausing to look back, he was startled to discover that the glen had disappeared. For as far as he could see there was nothing but the unbroken flatness of the plain. He tried to retrace his steps, but the dell was gone, as if it had never existed. Hathor felt the pouch he carried—his pan and book and sifter were still there. And his body, only yesterday a ruined thing, was almost healthy again. *Something* had happened there—magic.

He too hoped that magic would protect him when he entered the palace whose people had treated him so cruelly. For there was no deceit in Hathor, no cleverness or cunning. He picked out the high dome of Dripping Hall standing bladeless above its lesser relatives, and he simply walked toward it. Kneadmora had told him he would fight the queen's champion, so he would march right in and declare his challenge, when others might hesitate for fear of capture. That was his way, the only way he could survive among the devious humes. Perhaps it was the look of determination on his face, or perhaps it was the cloak of magic that had made the dell disappear, or was it the fine chopping axe that was Kneadmora's other gift to him? In any case, no one bothered him as he approached the castle. It was early yet, but already the road was increasingly crowded with other travelers. Hathor overheard a fat peddler telling another of the queen's arrival and the foreshortened market of the previous day.

"I crated all my goods again and brought them home, rather than risk the thieves of the town."

"I too. As if our lives were not hard enough."

"I hear she is looking for an escaped slave. Imagine, all this commotion over one lost animal."

"A pity. If there is no market today I'm ruined."

"You exaggerate, cousin," the one merchant said to the other, and Hathor dropped off so as not to draw attention to himself. *So, she is here*, he noted with satisfaction. Everything Kneadmora had predicted was coming true. And Hathor thought: *Mine is not to question the ways of the gods, but only to do their bidding*, though he never could have expressed himself with such eloquence. He pulled down his hat over his fine red hair, the most he could think to do as a disguise. As a butcher he had attained an unwonted notoriety, but away from the killing ground he looked like just another country bumpkin come to the castle fair on market day to gawk and stare at the fineries displayed there, though his thick torso contrasted strongly with the Wind-Websters' slim, patrician figures and features.

As he approached the gate he caught sight of the black guard of the Queen of Ice, and he knew her to be within the wagon they surrounded. For Hathor understood that the queen ruled by fear, and therefore was herself loathe to enter for fear of retribution. Hate breeds hate. Uncertain whether to pass through the gate into Dripping Hall or wait for her to emerge, Hathor stood to one side as the stream of commerce passed by him. Wagonloads of slaves were again intermingled with carts of produce, baskets of grain and fruit, braces of partridge tied by their feet to poles, heaps of cloth and carpet, a dizzying array of goods to be bought, sold, or bartered. Just yards away, in the tent of Randil, the elf musician cousin of Endril's, the three were planning their strategy for confronting the queen.

"She is come to find Hathor, though she probably suspects that we are here too," Endril said deliberately. "If we could just get a clue as to where he is."

"It's kind of hard to miss him in a crowd, the big oaf," Cal said with rough affection. At this Randil, who had been idly sitting by playing a soft melody on a curved flute, perked up his ears and jumped into the conversation.

"A troll, you say? Big fellow with reddish hair and a dour expression?"

"That's him!" Bith cried excitedly.

"It must be the 'Weeping Butcher,' " said Randil, but none of them knew what he meant, so Randil told the story of the troll who cried while he slaughtered, how he had become an entertainment in Dripping Hall for a few days, then escaped and hadn't been seen since.

"They say he was driven mad," Randil finished.

"How cruel!" Bith protested, for she knew how much it must have pained Hathor to take the lives of innocent creatures when he himself had forsworn them as food.

"But yet—escaped! Great news!" said Cal, to him this meant they would soon have his formidable axe-wielding presence on their side.

"Don't be so sure," Endril cautioned. "Who knows where he might have fled? Our whole plan depends upon finding him—"

"We haven't got a plan yet," Cal fired back.

"We know that whatever we do, Hathor is the key," Endril said with surprising patience, ignoring Cal's outburst. "We can only hope that the madness was temporary, and that he hasn't run far off while possessed."

"It was several days ago now that he vanished," Randil added, further dampening their hopes of finding him. "But the Wind-Websters should have found him. They are greatly fond of tracking and stalking, and they have specially trained dogs for the job. He must have found an extraordinary hiding place if he's still around."

"Extraordinary, indeed. Remember, Caltus Talienson and Elizebeth of Morea," Endril addressed them by their formal names for the first time in a long time, "we are on a righteous quest, we should not fear failure—"

"Fear?" Cal bridled, but Endril continued unperturbed:

"But know that we are blessed with the favor of the gods—"

Again Cal broke in: "It seems to me we've done most of the fighting and winning on our own—"

"Indeed, it may seem that way, but who is to say that at a key moment in the fight the gods have not subtly intervened, throwing your enemy off balance with an imperceptible twist of the ankle so that you can run him through, straightening an errant shot from my bow so that it pierces my enemy's heart, or, who knows, perhaps sheltering Hathor when he needs it most. So let us thank the gods for their protection, and ask them to approve our venture today."

"Which ones?" Bith asked. "That undependable Vili has been nowhere to be seen, the mysterious Claviger's messenger showed up but I missed it because I was the medium—"

"It doesn't matter by what names you call them. Freya or Thor, Claviger or Vili, as long as you show devotion they will respond."

"A nice way of putting it," said Randil, who had been listening in. "And the best way of showing reverence is through music. Come, cousin, let us play a tune of thanksgiving, then we'll pipe a battle call for your young squire there, but softly, for the enemy surrounds you, and you are sorely outnumbered."

Endril dug out his snake-carved flute from his pack, and together they began to play a slow and solemn hymn on the pipes, each note drawn out, the flutes in counterpoint, and their notes seemed to rise to heaven.

Cal fidgeted and worried that the music would take all day, for he knew the propensity of elves for endless strains, but after a few minutes the song soared to an ethereal ending. Endril pronounced himself ready to proceed.

"Let's leave our supposed slaves here with Randil and take a look for ourselves at the inside of Dripping Hall. Cal, you'll have to enter without that—" Endril pointed to the sword whose pitted blade Cal was lovingly whetting with a stone. "We must maintain our disguise as traders until the propitious moment comes."

Cal protested, but mildly, for he knew Endril was right. They donned their merchants' outfits again. Before they left, Bith put a mild HIDE spell on the tent. It did not become invisible, but made it so none who passed by would think to inquire about it or come in. Even Cal felt its effects. He had forgotten his boot dagger, but when he tried to reenter the tent he found that he could not hold the thought.

"Blast it, Bith. I can't keep my mind straight around your hex. Fetch me my boot sheath and knife, will you? They're in my pack."

"Leave them," Endril warned, but Cal insisted that even a weak merchant has the right to defend himself. As Bith ducked inside to get the items for Cal, Endril noticed activity near the queen's entourage. From the midst of the commotion came the dull roar of a familiar voice, repeatedly calling for the queen to come out and fight. The horses of the black guard were wild with terror, and Endril knew that only one being could have that voice and cause that ruckus—their beloved Hathor!

Leaving Bith and Cal behind, Endril rushed to the scene.

There was Hathor, pacing within an ill-formed ring, surrounded by the near-frantic horses and the threatening lances of the guard.

"I thought your cousin said he had escaped," Bith said to Endril accusingly as she and Cal rushed up to join him, along with most of the encampment, now wakened by the disturbance.

"He had. He came back. He is no longer mad. Ah, 'tis fine to see those mighty arms again. Don't worry, all goes well. That troll is smarter than we gave him credit for, or else he has had good coaching from someone. Not even the Queen of Ice can refuse a challenge thus issued. She will have to send out her champion. Hathor has put the whole onus on himself. Just as the Claviger's spirit messenger predicted, the success of our mission depends upon Hathor."

A huge crowd soon gathered. Here was free entertainment, and the best kind for a mob, violent and bloody. Hathor was remembering his last fight against the unwilling Bog Man. What would his opponent be like this time? He did not have to wait long to find out. The crowd gasped as the door to the queen's carriage swung open and the queen herself emerged, her regal figure dressed in black.

"You see," Endril whispered to Cal, "she does exist." The queen raised her arms to indicate she would speak, and the crowd fell silent.

"So, troll, you have escaped my clutches and now foolishly you have come back to my embrace."

"I challenge you."

"Yes, yes, I know all about it. Fool. Do you think I go anywhere without my best warrior? He will rip you apart, then you will be useless to me, but if that is what you desire—" She clapped her hands. From a second, smaller wagon behind her own, several of her guards brought forth her charge, surrounding him with upraised shields, hiding him from view until with a vicious roar the queen's champion entered the ring. At first glance Hathor thought: *It is a white bear!* But no, it was a bearlike creature with a white coat of fur but a nearly human face, except for the bearish muzzle and fangs. Hathor had seen bears before, but they had been mangy and poorly cared for, and they galumphed around clumsily, teetering when they tried to stand. This was a sleek, muscled beast, upright and erect, pacing lightly on padded paws that displayed sharp claws. It was easily a foot taller than Hathor. The animal's trainers were having trouble restraining it from tearing across the ring at Hathor immediately. As Hathor watched the magnificently wild bear ripping at its double leash, he felt admiration, pity, and a strange camaraderie, for he been treated the same way only days ago. He thought of the many times in the past weeks he had cleft the neck of an innocent creature with an axe like the one he held now. And he knew that he could not fight or kill this half bear.

"I will free it," Hathor decided, though that would make his task of defeating the queen more difficult. Speaking to the bear thing in the little bear talk he knew, and that the language of a very different sort of bear, Hathor said: "I do not fight."

"I fight for life," the beast answered with a fierce snarl. To the crowd it sounded as though the two combatants were merely growling at each other.

"Fight with me and not against me and I will see you free."

"Why do you not smell of blood in the mouth?" growled the bear, for it had smelled the troll and not found the telltale scent of meat on his breath.

"I know a better way," Hathor answered.

"Not for me," it snapped, and without warning it lunged at Hathor and the two engaged. Hathor's instincts took over and he countered the bear's rush, throwing up his hands to protect his face from the unsheathed claws that raked about his head. The bear was larger and stronger than Hathor, and it had the will to kill.

The crowd screeched and howled its delight as they grappled, but three of the watchers eyed each other grimly and wondered what they should do. Endril raised a hand of caution when Cal indicated his intent to crash the ring and fight alongside his long-lost companion. With only his dagger, Cal was overmatched in any case. But Hathor seemed strangely reluctant to fight—several times Cal, grunting and twisting his body as he watched the tussle, saw opportunities for Hathor to gain purchase or use his grinding teeth, yet he held back. Bith noticed too.

"He's not trying," she whispered to Cal.

The young hero nodded agreement. "The bear will outlast him."

Head to head now, Hathor felt the hot savage breath of the bear in his face. A confusing mass of emotions swept through Hathor even as he fought. His will to survive clashed with his loathing of killing any living thing. The bear, like any animal in a fight, sensed its opponent's indecision and pressed its attack. One swipe of a paw on Hathor's back tore away most of the flesh as if he had been flayed repeatedly. Stunned and bleeding, Hathor stumbled backward. Rolling its weight forward it shoved Hathor to the ground and placed its full weight on Hathor's shoulders with its two forepaws. One of the queen's guard strode forward, unsheathing his sword to deliver the final blow to the defeated troll. This was too much for Cal. With a furious yell he leapt into the ring and overtook the black guard, catching him before he had fully withdrawn his blade and stabbing him dead with a single thrust beneath the heart. The bear thing, sensing an opportunity to escape, jumped up from Hathor and crashed through the opening where the unattended horse of the slain guard reared up in fright. The crowd shrieked and fled in all directions. Hathor wobbled to his feet and embraced Cal, but then the black guards attacked. Endril ran to Randil's tent and returned with the seventeen villagers, pushing their way through the still fleeing mob to join the battle, Sheerstrake at their lead, sprinting wildly in his hurry to take his revenge. Bith, uncertain what to do, eased her way toward the carriage of the queen, who had withdrawn within at the first sign of trouble. Her questing mind came up against an indiscernible wall—Bith knew it must be a SHIELD spell like the one she had just used on Randil's tent. But this was something more, an impenetrable barrier that Bith could not pierce. The black carriage was for all intents in another world from the chaos of battle that raged outside its shell.

That contest was taking an interesting turn. Cal expected the mercenary troops of the Wind-Websters to come pouring out of the gate to Dripping Hall at any minute, but instead they barricaded that selfsame portal and remained within, peering out from slit windows high on the conical palace. The queen had tried to make allies through greed and intimidation, but the mercenaries felt no special loyalty to her. Moreover, they were not eager to challenge the troll whom they had tormented only recently, who now swung his axe overhead and fended off half a dozen of the black guard at a time.

Cal had taken up the halberd of a fallen enemy and kept another several at bay to the left. Then Endril led the villagers in a counterattack. Two dozen slaves, mostly humans, had grabbed clubs or the weapons of the fallen guards and joined in the fight. He had instructed them to swing for the sensitive noses of the horses, which sent them into a panic and further scattered the guard. Some of the guard were seen stripping off their distinctive black clothing and slipping into the mob, which continued to mill around in a frenzy, especially after the way into the safety of the palace was barred. The villagers, doubly inspired by revenge, fought well and soon encircled the remaining guards. A terrible slaughter would have ensued had not the villagers restrained the slaves and pulled a bloody Sheerstrake from the fight. The reunited four and their small force were masters of the battlefield. They met before the carriage, amid the littered carnage of war. Bith kissed Hathor on the cheek. Endril slapped him on the shoulder, and Cal, Cal need do nothing, for the two had just been fighting back-to-back in the old way. A grateful gaze between them affirmed the deep warrior bond.

"The four—together again!" Cal crowed. "We have much to tell thee, Hathor."

"Me too," Hathor grunted. "But where is the queen?"

Bith pointed to the wagon. "She's cloaked herself in a spell. I can't break it."

The last of the black guard had surrendered to the villagers, fearing the now-growing number of slaves who had armed themselves. The merchants and their retinues, fearing the beginning of a long siege, packed up their goods and soon clogged all roads away from Dripping Hall. All that remained behind were the victors, their prisoners, including several wounded and dying guards, and the imposing black wagon, still sheathed by magic.

A messenger bearing the pennant of the "king's peace" emerged from the gate of Dripping Hall and approached the four. He was not a mercenary but one of the Wind-Websters, a stately-looking elder with a pained expression dominating those usually blank features. Humility did not come easily to a Wind-Webster.

"The Council asks your terms. We remind you that we have a source of water within and are prepared to withstand a protracted siege."

Cal answered for the four. "We have no intention of laying siege to your worthless tower. Tell us how we can pry open this coach and kill the queen." Such cowards, he thought, their guards outnumbered his small band two to one and they feared a siege.

"Can't the butcher open it?" the Wind-Webster asked with a trace of a smile despite the tenseness of the moment.

"It is magic, fool," Cal shot back, enjoying the role of victor setting terms. "These are my conditions. First, send out a party to fetch the wounded and the dead. Second, forswear the slave trade now and forever more. Last, divulge to us the secrets of the queen. Then we will leave. Now go!"

"Goodness, when did you think of all that?" Bith exclaimed when the Wind-Webster passed from earshot.

"When I heard last night how they treated Hathor," said Cal. "But let's get to the immediate problem." He turned to the wagon, raised his borrowed halberd, and brought down a crashing blow, but the lance broke without touching the paneled wood. Hathor threw his considerable bulk against the unseen shield, but he merely bounced off and fell to the ground.

Even Endril was daunted. "This is so frustrating," he said. "We have her but we don't have her."

"Those Websters had better produce an answer for us," Cal warned, "or I'll siege them like they've never been sieged before, with flaming arrows and catapults of hot pitch, and worse—"

"You won't have to wait long for their response," Endril pointed out sagely. "Here comes the emissary of the defeated now."

The Wind-Webster looked even unhappier than before. Behind him were a dozen men bearing litters to remove the wounded and dying black guards. Cal ordered the healthy prisoners kept for the time being, though he had no intention of taking them anywhere. Then he addressed the representative of the Wind-Websters.

"I see that you have met my first demand that you take care of the fallen in battle. What about the second and third requirements? Well? Will you desist from your vile practice of procuring serfs by purchase? And will you help us rid the world and yourselves of the evil Queen of Ice? What is your reply?"

"The Council says—we promise to forswear the buying of slaves in favor of paying wages to those who do our work. But as to the queen, we know no way to penetrate her magic. Indeed, she has held us under sway for years now. We are helpless before her, and therefore cannot help you." The emissary sounded unsure as to whom he hoped would win the battle outside their walls.

"You must free the slaves you own now, as well, and allow them the choice of returning to their homes or accepting your salaries," said Cal, as always looking out for the ordinary man. "Now, withdraw, and do not open the gates of Dripping Hall until I order you to do so." Thoroughly abashed, the Wind-Webster retreated with the litter-bearers to wait out the resolution of the impasse.

Bith walked round and round the wagon, probing and testing with her mind, but she could find no weakness in the enchanted covering.

"I must go back to the words of the Claviger again," Endril mused. "It is Hathor who must solve this dilemma. What do you think, my big friend?"

This was a new sensation for Hathor, being asked not to lift something heavy or chop a load of tree limbs for the fire or swing his axe in battle, but to help by thinking! He looked back on all he had learned in his captivity, of the lessons Kneadmora had taught him, and of how he knew now that the queen's evil plan and his own personal torment were one and the same. He had overcome his temptation, now it only remained to thwart the queen's designs.

He thought and he thought but little entered his huge head. He began to daydream, and in his reverie he envisioned himself as a little boy, playing at the troll children's game of Sticks and Rocks. "Rocks beat sticks," he mumbled to himself, his rough hands childishly pantomiming the gestures that accompanied the rhymes. "Ice cracks rocks," he resumed, remembering with fondness the pudgy trollish faces of his boyhood companions. Then in a flash he remembered why he was remembering and stood up and shouted aloud: "Fire melts ice!"

His companions were startled by his sudden outburst, but

Endril as usual grasped the meaning of the thing before anyone else.

"Quickly! Gather wood, all you can find. 'Fire melts ice,' indeed, wise Hathor. Now hurry, scavenge the battlefield for wood, cloth, anything that will burn. Leave a skeleton guard with the prisoners and send the villagers and others out too. We need all the fuel we can muster to melt this one's cold, cold heart!"

Hathor beamed with pride as a hundred humes scurried around in search of firewood. He turned to look at the carriage wherein was the one who had threatened the land and tortured him. He wondered if she could hear them in their preparations, even see the mound growing that would be her funeral pyre.

"I thought of it, me, Hathor!" he said, and he did a clumsy dance of joy, those big feet shaking the earth as he rollicked about. Soon there surrounded the carriage a tremendous pile of refuse from the battle, abandoned carts hacked to bits, tents ripped to shreds and dipped in oil, even logs. Someone had found a load of wooden wind-loom blades, immense and well lacquered—they would burn excellently!

Cal held aloft a torch. Addressing the queen, he shouted: "Come out or meet your doom, to burn within like the witch you are!" Silence met his call. "Come forth and we will spare you. Elsewise, I set this torch to the heap!" Again his words went unanswered. He was about to give her a third and final warning when Bith, who had been strangely silent through the proceedings, sprang forward, took the torch from him, and cast it instantly onto the stack that exploded into flame.

"Never give a witch three chances," she said. "It's very bad luck."

The flames raced around the circular mass and soon the carriage was engulfed. Or was it? It was impossible to see through the smoke and flames whether or not the shield had melted and the wagon was really on fire. Then as they watched helplessly, the roof of the wagon blew off, and the Queen of Ice appeared above the carriage, riding on the back of one of her vile winged creatures, an enormous slizard that she must have kept inside with her all along. Hathor flung his axe skyward futilely and Endril managed a couple of near misses from his bow, but she flew off with a shrill scream that the wind-whipped flames muffled, her royal black gown streaming behind her. She had escaped!

"We have lost!" Hathor yelled in frustration.

"No, Hathor, we have won. The queen has retreated to her lair. She has lost most of her guard, and the alliance of the Wind-Websters, we've seen to that. We can never hope to completely conquer evil," Endril philosophized.

"No, but we have driven it back. Look!" Bith cried, and she pointed to the Mistwall. The rip was sealing itself, and the Wall looked weakened and thinner, less threatening. The cold north wind that had threatened to sweep south was again contained behind the Mistwall, as it should be. They had drained the power of the queen until she could no longer hold open the Mistwall for her frigid invasion.

"I guess there'll be spring in our land after all," said Cal. "We ought to think about getting back there for it." The men of the village of Steadfast-by-Sea let out a yell of agreement to that.

So it was that Hathor the Butcher became Hathor the Baker, and saved the country to the south from a wintry fate. The good troll and his companions were praised in song and skald, as Hathor once wished. The evil Queen of Ice vanished, the Wind-Websters were reformed, and the land knew peace. The men of Steadfast-by-Sea returned to their homes and families. Together again with his three outcast companions, Hathor trudged south, dreaming of his cozy cave on the banks of the River Drasil and the oven he would build there. "Ach," he said to himself, "life is hard, but life is good. I will bake bread."

EXTRAORDINARY ADVENTURES
by *New York Times* bestselling author
PIERS ANTHONY

The Apprentice Adept Series—Welcome to the astonishing parallel worlds of Phaze and Proton. Where magic and science maintain an uneasy truce. And where Mach, a robot from Proton, and his alternate self, magical Bane from Phaze, hold the power to link the two worlds—or destroy them completely.

＿OUT OF PHAZE 0-441-64465-1/$4.95
＿ROBOT ADEPT 0-441-73118-X/$4.95
＿PHAZE DOUBT 0-441-66263-3/$4.95
＿UNICORN POINT 0-441-84563-0/$4.50

The Books of Tarot—On the planet Tarot, nothing is real. Or everything. For the shimmering *Animation* curtains move across the worldscape like a storm of monsters, changing fantasy into reality—and trapping the wanderer-monk Paul in a nightmare of dragons, demons...and lusts!

＿GOD OF TAROT 0-441-29470-7/$4.50
＿VISION OF TAROT 0-441-86461-9/$3.95
＿FAITH OF TAROT 0-441-22565-9/$4.95

Bio of an Ogre—Piers Anthony's remarkable autobiography! A rich, compelling journey into the mind of a brilliant storyteller. "Fascinating!"—*Locus*

＿BIO OF AN OGRE 0-441-06225-3/$4.50